# THE BLUE BOOKS

A Book
Turn of a Pang
French Kiss, or, A Pang's Progress

Nicole Brossard

Coach House Books

first edition of *The Blue Books*

Published with the assistance of the Canada Council for the Arts and the Ontario Arts Council

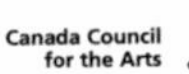

Coach House Books also thanks the Canada Council for the Arts for assistance for the original translations of these books in 1976 and 1986.

NATIONAL LIBRARY OF CANADA CATALOGUING IN PUBLICATION

Brossard, Nicole, 1943-
The blue books : A book, Turn of a pang, French kiss, or, A pang's progress / Nicole Brossard ; translated by Larry Shouldice (A book) and Patricia Claxton (Turn of a pang, French kiss).

Translation of: *Un livre, Sold-out, French kiss : étreinte-exploration.*

ISBN 1-55245-120-8

I. Shouldice, Larry, 1945- II. Claxton, Patricia, 1929- III. Title. IV. Title: Book / Nicole Brossard. V. Title: Turn of a pang. VI. Title: French kiss, or, A pang's progress.

PS8503.R7A274 2003 C843'.54 C2003-901379-0
PQ3919.2.B765A274 2003

To Barbara Godard, who first introduced my books to Coach House Press and who has been since a perspicacious reader and translator of my work.

– N.B.

## Contents

## An Introduction

by Nicole Brossard
translated into English by Susanne de Lotbinière-Harwood

The intention here is not to go back in time, but rather to touch once again the energy which, from 1965 to 1975, coursed through the bodies and ways of thinking of a generation. To retrace the writing pleasures animating my thoughts at a time when I was reading Hubert Aquin's *Prochain Episode*, Marshall McLuhan's *The Gutenberg Galaxy*, *Les Larmes d'Éros* by George Bataille and *Le Degré zéro de l'écriture* by Roland Barthes. A time when the only Canadian writers I could name were Montréalers Leonard Cohen, Mordecai Richler and Irving Layton. Pink Floyd was my favourite group and the films that mattered to me were directed by Pasolini, Visconti, Fellini and Antonioni. Along with two more *made in the U.S.A.*: *Citizen Kane* and *Rebel Without a Cause*. A noticeably male world.

Back then, twentysomethings were agents of change all over the world. One part of the freedom we sought was located at the level of the solar plexus; another was wholly wrapped up in the unfathomable dimension of the pleasure of the text; yet another wanted to change the world, especially to reinvent Québec, to pull it out of clericalism and of alienation. There was a body of literature to discover, to make known and to write: thus was born the review *La Barre du Jour*, to change the landscape of the land of snow into an urban one made of words.

Writing was a way to appropriate the world. This needed doing at all costs. Language had to be made malleable, mobile, fluid, able to withstand all experimentations, all stripping away; to be cut up into a thousand fragments, its Greek and Latin roots exposed; to be stretched and compressed so as to reveal the thousand facets of desire, the varieties of meanings and emotions. As well, writing was to help demystify the myths generative of exploitation and alienation. The world was still real and literature had meaning, had the irresistible flavour of renewal and knowledge. Everything I intuited, though I hadn't the words to express it, vigorously drove me towards poetry but also towards fiction, into that disturbing zone where the unimaginable and the unthinkable find, if not an explanation, then at least a haven compatible with the vertigo at their source.

In 1974, in *French Kiss*, I wrote: 'for a polemical existence.' This expression no doubt rather accurately summarizes that complex feeling which, starting with my very first books, was to include the playful dimension of writing, the commitment to struggle (subversion, rupture, transgression) and, also, underlying the idea of literature as an ethics, the certainty that, although it was a space conducive to the wildest imaginings, literature provided lucidity, made humans even more human – that is, compelled them to dream of a life and of passions that could set them free and lead them away from stupidity and violence.

*A Book* put to work my fascination for the acts of writing and reading, *Turn of a Pang* sought to revive the Montréal of my childhood superimposed with the cultural and political present of seventies Québec through 'a trumped-up tale with varied reflections in avalanche (presuming snow) ... ' And *French Kiss, or, A Pang's Progress* synthesized Montréal as a metaphor for ludic writing, urban life, the French language 'frenchkissing' a sexed/sexual tongue available for any and all adventures involving knowledge and imagination. When Marielle drives crosstown from east to west along Sherbrooke Street in her old Plymouth, aka 'Violet,' it is 'a carousel of history and geography,' it is about straddling grammar and going off to explore the inner recesses of the images and life irrigating the brain. Having grown up in the west end of Montréal, I was always intensely captivated by the Francophone east end of the island. The east represented a kind of delinquency and freedom that attracted me. The east was mysterious, dangerous; it had bars and clubs and gangs. It was also where a colloquial language was spoken, one rich with affect, vivid, a language in which I recognized a belonging we were forbidden to acknowledge: a Québec that was colonized and for this very reason in need of transformation.

The visual aspect plays an important role in each one of these three novels: graffiti, comics, calligraphy, headlines, typeface changes are used to reinforce the transgression and to emphasize the work of the reading eye which, beginning with *Suite logique* (1970) up to my latest novel, *Hier* (2001), has always been a core element. Reading is eye-opening: opening one's eyes onto the world, desiring it, questioning it.

Each one of these books also contains a geography of bodies and characters instead of a quest and a surrender through them (this came later, with *Mauve Desert* [1987], *Baroque at Dawn* [1995] and *Hier* [2001]). So, resistance to a novelistic imperative is strongest and most radical in my first three novels, as if I had had to refuse to play the game of referential illusion in order to keep only the extra-textual, attracted and motivated, in short, by the inexpressible, the *hot* dimension of semantic arousal. Everything that could be clearly and easily expressed – such as 'Once upon a time' or 'It was a dark and stormy night' – was graphically framed and bore the ironic title of chapter. The 'chapter' phenomenon would be reproduced in each of my subsequent novels, taking up progressively more and more space, like in *Picture Theory*, with its chapter entitled 'Emotion,' then with the first fifty pages of *Mauve Desert*; however, it does seem that no matter how much space is yielded to novelistic *make-believe*, the logic of my novels always ends up being disrupted by another project: translation in *Mauve Desert*, theatre in *Hier*.

What do the memories of the books one has written look like? I believe they resemble what we become with each and every instance of surrender, each and every act of resistance invested in existing through them. Certainly, the memories of books one has written often correspond to the era that brought them into being. The seventies were turbulent times – bold, political, free and especially full of hope. So, reception of these books was split between offended official critics and informal reviews by writers open to a new approach to the novel.

As I write this introduction, I'm curious about revisiting a form of writing emblematic of my resistance to narrative. A resistance which, by not coercing the 'I' to bear witness, grants it the full range of possibilities for exploration, surprise, astonishment, play, reconfiguration of meaning. I believe the same principle applies to eroticism as well as to the sexual encounters between characters, 'attractive signalling figures.' Living in the slipstream of words, living in the obsession of words as one lives in the obsession of sex as metaphor for an inexpressible lust for life. There's no coincidence in the fact that both *Turn of a Pang* and *French Kiss* are subtitled 'embrace' in their original French editions. This attests the importance, in my eyes, of the spark that goes off at the moment of embracing, of writing and of reading: creative current, major sensation, emotional thought-form.

The world has changed. Fiction has in part gone over to reality. And reality, as we know, is now an industry. Another part of fiction morphed into autobio/fiction at the speed of a *me descending the staircase of daily life*. Another one perpetuates the work of writers seeking new spaces within language as a place to deploy their quest for meaning and the old 'dur désir de durer' (Éluard). One thing is certain: the much sought-after thrill anticipated as outcome of the formal performance has now replaced emotion. The present, so prized in my texts as a time for contemplation and lucidity, is from now on a tautological present. The body (a theme my generation cherished above all else and hastened to associate with the pleasure, disorders and impulses connected with writing), the body, from here on fragmented right down to its genes, is today an installation, an object, a veritable shopping mall. And so, what of our humanity? If indeed the meaning we assign to life, to people and to words is what constantly modifies its configuration, then what can it possibly look like in a time when we increasingly find ourselves using the expression 'post-humanity'? The stakes are not slight. They no doubt require more than ever an unequivocal fervour for language and everything it brings into our experience, with or without our consent: 'She rides eager astride the delible ink … ', 'Awkward grammar … ' (C. Bök).

December 31, 2002

# A Book

by Nicole Brossard
translated by Larry Shouldice

*A Book* is a translation of *Un livre*, which was first published in 1970 by Editions du Jour.



This translation was first published as *A Book* in 1976 by Coach House Press as part of the Quebec Translations series, edited by Barbara Godard and Frank Davey.

## I

A text beginning like this
or
the beginning of this text which will bring about the revelation of several attitudes which happen to have been noticed in the past few hours.
Routes to be followed.
Which draw away from certain observation points, which are in no way essential to the arrangement of spaces between which two three and more women and men come to life from without or within become characters, which is to say the usual setting.
The text and several variables.
These few days past women and men touching one another in the crowd inevitably were observed and their participation sought.
The text and the spaces.
Because if O.R. and Dominique have lived together for five years their existence depends principally on those empty times during which they have been busy just being. They love each other: each being able to live without the other.
They emerge in the midst of recorded space and their present and future attitudes cannot be presumed.

## 2

Is it plan or challenge? No matter, since the words come one by one to claim their place at the centre of this narrative, and since there is no need for successes or failures to be indicated, any more than there is for the voice of desire to be heard in the variables and the spaces. O.R. and Dominique have little to say to anyone else. And to each other. … when the words outstrip reality, and even fiction, it is time for them to be silenced.

The words revolve around the variables, namely: is a description or general narration enough to produce anything more than something else, another pale thing. The variables taken as persons. Variables in the crowd, persons in the crowd and life comes to life, but no one knows it.

## 3

Thus when you get over thinking about its five letters the crowd becomes this soft silly thing that hints of pleasure and other sorts of thrills, a vague and indefinite place to which the eye and heart are drawn as easily as to a strange body lying in the shadows, a good spot for arranging a rendezvous. Thus the point of meeting is both the entire crowd and this flashing light at the intersection of hundreds of variables.

Between O.R. and Dominique plus three others there is a tacit agreement: to remain available and not to depend on anyone. O.R. in the crowd hardly stands out among the variables. O.R.: to be able to reply with unusual gestures to the words of others. O.R., happy and strong in her flesh.

## 4

Variable.
Between eight and nine o'clock while the three others are waiting, O.R. and Dominique are moving calmly along the warm pavement of Saint-Hubert Street. Mixed with the crowd, with the others, the same as the others, they await the moment of meeting. Soon they are the meeting.
In the text.
O.R. and Dominique follow along their way, their route under the same kind of lighting that allows the words to shine out and be restored one by one, precisely, imprecisely, according to the obscure laws of chance.
The three others resemble them. They too are this meeting. Five meeting points. Dominique: to desire nothing, but to understand. The three others unanimous. O.R. silent.

5

Any other variable would only be a matter of words. A matter of words that has been lived, which takes form from nothing, from little, from two or three words and which finally takes over the space completely, in the book as elsewhere. From the page to the book time builds up its banalities, leaving little space for attempts at seduction.

O.R. can only be continually revived and regilded. Like her coat of arms, which the words greet with pleasure between two dull periods. From one variable to another, the narrative is there only as an intermediary, used by the force of things – all of which remain to be described when it comes to putting them to the test. It is the same with O.R. and her relations with the others. Each of them always requires an intermediary.

O.R. attentive, Dominique too. The doors of the restaurant are closed. It is day. The others left at dawn.

## 6

It is day. The crowd takes some time to reappear. Sun. It is sunny. Exhausted, O.R. walks slowly beside Dominique who steers her toward the métro. Dominique: words and days look alike … when they are added up … with their effectiveness subtracted … they let you stop for a while if you want.

Later.

O.R. stretched out on the bed, half asleep. Dominique in front of her, an absent look on his face.

Not much to write about O.R. and Dominique after lovemaking.

Rather a few notes in the margin of their sleep.

Parenthesis

while the text continues and clarifies its emergence as event.

Parenthesis in the core of each of the characters.

## 7

Several things are expressed this way: are thus written in the margin. And essential as they are, they interest no one. The marginal notes are invaluable. Invaluable in the same way as those characters of whom little is said and who, by the simple fact of their existence, pollute or purify, ratify the air that is breathed by the others, by the ones who are named and narrated for the unacknowledged purpose of making plausible what looks like fact in the marginal notes.

O.R., at five o'clock in the afternoon, with a cup of tea. Her hands around it. Attentive. Naked. Crushing heat.

Description: perhaps, but O.R. would not emerge from it alive. Dead rather (like something else).

## 8

From all appearances, O.R. resembles the others. But how?
O.R. sitting on the balcony, nude. For a few minutes only, because of the passersby who look up and frown.
Others too who greet her, waving with their index and middle fingers in the shape of a V. More and more variables gather under the balcony. Multicoloured variables, and soon some blue ones. Words no longer have the same meaning. O.R. has nothing to say, and Dominique is doing the talking. A conversation between the deaf. Still, they leave them alone. It is too hot to arrest anyone.
Variable.
The five o'clock crowd and this woman sitting naked on a balcony. Too pretty, ugly, vulgar, whorish. Strangely the words accumulate but do little more than accumulate.
O.R. is already into another space. Dominique knows it.

## 9

Dominique: outside of us? O.R.: no one. On a green plot of ground named Mount Royal – naming the surroundings before silencing them and belonging to them. Living here at the very moment when things are becoming intimate and an unknown joy is being born in the silence. Untellable tomorrow – in the sun, O.R. and Dominique, stretched out. Their eyes closed as if with pleasure. Eyelids fluttering because there is the pleasure of being there and waiting for nothing.

Unmoving, seen this way by Mathieu who is watching them from a distance, staring at them, unmoving.

Time precious and inexplicable, a note in the margin.

## 10

The end of one stage: starting the cycle of words again. If everything were to be said again, identical, the following pages would have no other existence than in their white surfaces. But the cycle is not a perfect repetition in that it allows for several variables, variables which always suggest the possibility of total renewal.
And so O.R. and Dominique got up early this morning.

II

Reading O.R. is the same as reading Dominique and Mathieu because all three play identical roles in the book as routine machines of awareness. Reading (not facts and actions, but) O.R., Dominique and Mathieu must be seen as an essentially entertaining process: the eye reacts to the most minute stimuli NOTICE noticed *awakening* Joy something like that but even more so in the continuity of the writing.

Reading: or sorting out the black mass of words, reading as though you were writing another's words as they appear and move through your vision.

O.R., sitting on the floor, cross-legged, with a book on her lap. A book she is not reading. But which she is touching. Dominique and Mathieu, face to face, bend over an impromptu game of go, each anxious to manoeuvre himself into the winning space.

## 12

O.R. and Mathieu seen together for the first time by Dominique, who is touched. Sheets, bed and bedroom as space and surface, as description. Actions performed and being performed, nothing that could be written without being *in*significant. Dominique's head leaning on O.R.'s shoulder. Mathieu's head on her lap: a triangle formed in silence and tenderness.

## 13

The words always follow each other quite closely. It is easy to see them and read them, but the eye is quickly clouded by the desire to know even before the eyes have read, to have read without reading, to read before and after. Before through the memory and after through speculation. Thus it is rarely at the right time that the eye does the reading it is supposed to do.

Between the lines and the words

the spaces reveal as much as the text. If not more, if not the essence. Each line distracts because it evokes an other place that is attractive, but generally harmful because alien to what really matters (?). This elsewhere, this distraction, has been created by O.R., Dominique and Mathieu. Not because they exist but because someone is telling about them and others are there to build them up or tear them down.

## 14

This somewhere else is made that much more interesting by mystery, violence and strangeness, which have proven to be sure weapons against boredom.

A TROUBLED ATMOSPHERE

*O.R. had made this move in order to thwart Dominique. She knew that sooner or later he would come begging her to get rid of Mathieu. Only she could make the ultimate move that would set them both free, though not for the same reasons.*

*Dominique had come back. Strange, his face ashen he sat down in the red armchair in the livingroom. O.R. came over to him and provocatively asked the one question he was waiting for but which never should have been asked.*

OR ANOTHER WHICH READS THUS:

*Dominique would go to meet O.R. at the agreed time. He would pretend to flirt with all the girls so that after a few minutes of this little game, she would leave the discotheque and of course bump right into Mathieu who, after a few minutes' discussion, would see her home. Thus if everything went according to plan, Mathieu would never ask for even a cent back from Dominique who, having thus paid off his debt so easily, could at last leave the country and go start a new life somewhere else.*

## 15

Dominique, stretched out on the balcony with a glass of beer in his hand, O.R., inside, clipping her toenails. Street noises, especially trucks at this time of the morning. Dominique: get up and go give O.R. a kiss on the neck. O.R.: goddamned toenails.

The event is seen from a distance and out of context. All that is happening is this reading being done, the only real thing, causing a few muscles to move imperceptibly and making one conscious of his own breathing.

## 16

The present tense is everything that gathers together spontaneously and lives without any intermediary. In direct relation. The immediate. Like those characters whose only role is to be attentive and present.

In a text in the present the synthesis is done by itself, for nothing can adequately maintain a description of what the eye sees, the hand touches, or the flesh desires and dreams of.

The present, when it monopolizes the whole body, abolishes the past and never allows the future to encroach upon its time.

O.R. in the streaming water of the shower, squirming happily.

## 17

Mathieu alone, in a Snack Bar at midnight, sitting on a stool, his head turned toward the waitress. Heat. Sweat rolling down most of his body. The waitress barely moving. The radio, music. Then an extraordinary boom about five hundred feet from the restaurant. Dead silence. Sirens. People rushing up. Mathieu can't keep from smiling. Rumours are flying. Dominique at the exit of a cinema, in the neon light, holding a bus ticket in his teeth. O.R. out with Dominique C. in an English part of the city. The night goes on and on.

The others are seen in the distance, damp, crushed by the heat and by sleep.

The present discontinuous as soon as the variables appear.

## 18

Something else tonight as well.
O.R. and the evening's shared places and scenes.
O.R. breaking free of the happy bonds of the present. Thinking of other things. Of the meetings in Hampstead, in the stronghold of Judge Magnate, O.R. restless, aggressive, helpless. Words and situation: *Yes or no*. The text versus the temptation to tell it all. O.R. upset because all evening it has been a question of others through herself. Because she is part of a group that is perishing, slowly, on their backs with their legs apart. O.R. and Dominique C. sharing their revolt. Which is subsiding. Blending gently into the caresses of two women, shared with the tips of their fingers, their tongues.

## 19

The experience of words, of the discontinuous, is inevitable. Now and then the variables are intriguing, enough to distract any character and make him renew contact with the past, or to involve him in the future.

*Yes or no. Better dead than …* (to be filled in).

## 20

And so O.R. and Dominique got up early this morning. A bit sad, but present and available.

The words hesitate before undertaking the rest, the next page. Another page on which they will reproduce, are already reproducing their story, of how they came to be.

## 21

Superfluous words: always in one's mind but impossible to write down in a sure, appropriate place. Superfluous words assembled in the margins. Characters who are in the text, but who remain backstage. Who are there as a pretext for the text to continue with no other goal than to keep telling of its genesis as life gradually takes form. Strange but plausible narration.
O.R., sitting at her work table, writing an open letter to the newspapers. On the topic of open letters. A form of literary participation in community life. O.R., bunched over the white paper, page, soon letter. A gratifying gesture: to write. O.R. visibly Dominique's target as he leans towards her. At the very moment she finishes and signs her letter.

## 22

A discontinuous text like the discontinuous life of thoughts and actions. A style of life and expression in which one rarely comes to the point. A mechanism that doesn't leave much time for understanding the spaces, voids, empty times, all of which are revealing.
And so O.R. and the others have been described at arbitrary moments, here and there when the words trade their letters for images.
O.R., Dominique and Mathieu are watching, hands full of popcorn, like modern seers. In the dark, the cinema half empty, half full. Atmosphere. On the screen, the others take on colour.

## 23

On the C.s' back lawn, Dominique stretched out on the grass between O.R. and Dominique C. About eight o'clock in the evening. All three are very calm. More than simple relaxation in their vegetal tranquility: a condition. Flush with the soil, the three of them lying with the earth against their backs. Eyelids closed.
Perhaps also.
O.R. and Dominique C. on either side of Dominique. Green all around. Private grounds. The C.s' garden. About eight o'clock in the evening. Lying on the earth. Three smiling corpses.
Lovers much later in the night.

24

O.R.: the fact of experiencing something different for once. Dominique: an experience. O.R.: the fact of feeling something as an enlargement or enrichment of awareness, knowledge, aptitudes. Dominique: an experience. O.R. on page 659 in the dictionary. Dominique, in the kitchen, busy cooking an egg: persevering. O.R. confronting words. Face to face. Word by word. A matter of words. An atmosphere being created half wordlessly in the warm afternoon of the month of July.

## 25

On each new page a new thing is preparing, attracting all attention, coming into being so that once more, once more are traced the shimmering and excessive lines of the manuscript. Immediately into the business of reading. And carried along by what follows.
But on the same page: O.R., between two rows of foodstuffs, is picking tins of preserves. Air conditioning. O.R., a shopping list in her hands. The metal, cold against the hand on the handle of the shopping cart. Cold hands. Goose flesh. The shopping list: simple words. Now with the cashier, the employee. Everyday life: problematical words.

## 26

In the kitchen, O.R., Dominique C., Mathieu, Dominique and Henri. Together again for the first time since their all-night session of drinking and discussing together. Sitting around the table with a large platter filled with fresh fruit. Elbows leaning on the edge of the table. Looking at each other in silence. Bursting into laughter.

The others are somewhere else.

The five of them. Brought together by a word, a figure. A unity which weighs in the existence of each of them. The night goes on, making its way through their words or the story ventures into metaphor: TITLE OF STORY. The story itself. Told in its title. Slowly, the night goes on.

They stay up in the white light of the kitchen, around the table, with the coffee pot.

## 27

They stay up all this time. Spend the whole night beside one another. Attentive but relaxed. Henri is reading poems by Miron. Starts the same ones several times. Henri's voice. The buzzing of a fly caught in the door screen. The text being read. The night goes on forever. Right through till dawn. They leave. O.R. and Dominique remain alone. Rain starts to fall.

28

To write the present passage. A passage which opens on nothing but the relative positions of a hand and eye and some paper. The passage from desired words to written words. A gesture which draws attention and concentrates it within a few sentences, hoping thus to attain various new dimensions in seeing.

Anything can be written, anything not essential, in this passage. Anything that can be said and which speaks from within can be inscribed and left as a testimony to the chance of time.

Any desired thing can be written. Only evidence, not having to be translated in the curved lines of language, is an exception to the rule of words. Evidence belongs to an other than literary order. Thus the writing of and perseverance in composing this text implies a bias for literature, for repetition.

## 29

Written things.
'Not much to say to each other. Not much to write ... ' Several times things gain importance in the text. Thing as a general term used to designate either a difficult reality to explain or a circumstance, a fact it would be superfluous to make specific.
Deep down in things
O.R. and Dominique are deep in sleep. The telephone ringing. Rain on the roof. Street noises. The telephone ringing.
The things come by themselves
in every sort of shape to warn us that it's time to open our eyes.
O.R. sitting on the edge of the bed. Dominique asleep in the damp sheets.

30

The page turned. From one end of the book to the other: 1. the space reserved for O.R. and the others. 2. the space necessary for the completion of the text.
The page turned, eyes anticipating the next chapter. The text goes on with the same characters and from time to time a few variables. In the text as elsewhere.
O.R. and Dominique got up early this morning. The rain a sign of a change in the weather. Different.

31

The production of a text.
Not much different from existing ones, but unique, unmatched. A single page of text. Written in the continuity of a mode of composition resembling others in the past, suggesting others to come.
The cancellation of one thing for the benefit of another. The text confronting the text's precipitousness. Words which take their meaning from other words at the expense of the characters, sketches of men and women made to remain such. Henri, apparently a stranger, in all these instances experienced by Mathieu, Dominique, O.R. and Dominique C. But. Henri in the text in the same regard as the others. A character.

32

Henri in a space.
The text: Henri alone, Henri in a crowd. Himself a variable among the others. On Saint-Denis Street. At four o'clock in the afternoon, in the rain. In the grayness. A passerby like the others. Different because he is named and inscribed in the text.
The life of a text. Life through a text. A different reality. Taking on importance because it becomes the centre of attraction, because attention is focused on a specific man, his private life.

## 33

*Henri's private life.*
Henri alone in his room. Listening. Music. A private life. A life which is temporarily taking place in a vacuum. Comfortably. Intimate with things, with his flesh. Aware. Henri in the present. Selfish and in love at the same time.
Private life: since the others are extravagant and gradually fill up the space (in cubic feet) needed for their highly intimate actions. Private ... lives of others, their words, personalities, pretenses. Their affection also.
Henri in the privacy of his room. Eyes wide open. No comparison. Wide open: a seer.

## 34

*Henri's words.*

Few, but full of consequence. Because political. Words within everyone's reach. Clear and precise. Exposing corruption, provoking reactions for better or worse. Henri beyond problematical words. In this sense, engaged in history, in the trajectory of inordinate actions. Words which have nothing to do with this text: necessary words, prerequisites which need continually to be repeated.

Henri's words are the first on others' blacklists. Action words that repetition has made even more caustic. Troubled words. Indispensible words. Henri with words on the floor of the Maurice Richard arena, this twelfth evening of the month of July. In the heat and sweat. Elsewhere than in the text.

35

Henri in the text, between the words. A character revealed after several pages of writing but present from the very first lines in the book.

Note.

Henri at the florist's. Surrounded by flowers, stems, ferns. A smell, they say, of death. Sweet death, surely a happy death. At the florist's. Air conditioning. Flowers in the coolness, they say, embalm the air. Henri, his hand on the green of the rose stem which smells of rose and distracts him. Which smells of rose and makes him happy. At the florist's, a rose is not yet a rose. The red rose: the folly of grandeur (esthetics in the colour) obvious in these words.

## 36

The night is as long as a comparison endlessly being written and taking form in the sentence.
The ritual of slowly sipped coffee. The words rare. The long night in the yellow light of the kitchen. At O.R. and Dominique's place. All five of them sitting around the table. Exhausted. But determined.
The words gather in the margin. A very strong impression of living beyond things and words, of being extravagantly.
Henri, carrying a book, at dawn, in Lafontaine Park. His hands sweaty. Eyes full of tears. Henri walks in the park despite his fatigue and joy. Henri doesn't remember anything except the water at which he is looking at this instant.

## 37

The same day. Some five hours later. Henri stretched out on a bench in Lafontaine Park. His eyes open. Sweating profusely. Wanting to move, to be even hotter. Henri racing along Sherbrooke Street.
For ten minutes.
Henri in the shower. The water, pulsing, smooths the hair on his body, the water overrunning his body. Pleasure in the water. The telephone ringing.
The text retreating in this excerpt about Henri and things. The text outdistanced by events. Catching up with time and again beginning to show within its framework the painful distortions latent in any form of telling.

38

In Henri's room. O.R. and Dominique C. lying beside one another. Henri's kneeling above their bodies. Dominique C.'s lips. O.R.'s sex. Hands moving. Sexes stirring moist and glistening. Out of breath and life. Henri. The smell of the two women. Their caresses intensifying. Their beauty. Henri euphoric.

The bodies plunge into the vague terrains of the unknown, of knowledge. To write it: to witness it. A spectator. Witness: outside. Superfluous (cf. superfluous words … ; page 37).

The text without variables. The text, put off until later for phrasing. Unlikely to be read now. Waiting for the words to take charge again.

## 39

On the bus. A Sunday afternoon in July. The variables are rare. A few of them here and there, perspiring, collapsed on the green leather seats. It is all a matter of atmosphere: Henri at four o'clock this same afternoon, at the corner of Bleury and Sherbrooke streets. The colour of the buildings. Things alive and attractive. Life without any doubt. Reduced to its simplest expression, but in the text, complex, veiled in words, always somewhere else, unreal and excessively sought after. Always future and better.
Henri in the text: a helpless spectator.

## 40

The book today: being handled and examined. A trinket. The written object: a fictitious *ne plus ultra* that civilization sets clumsily aglitter for the unobservant but acquiescent looks of nonilliterates. The written object: dead. The power of death, its vertiginous power. Overpowering because there is nothing and no one impervious to the charm of written objects, dead objects.

The words turn around other words.

Henri sleeps soundly deep in his bed. Under the sheets. Covered from shoulder to foot. Henri in someone else's eyes. Looked at. Touched. Caressed by Dominique C.

## 41

The book takes shape.
The pages assemble, forming a rectangle (10"x 8"). A quarter inch of space and letters. The manuscript in a future book. Book-manuscript.
O.R. and Dominique look at each other, narcissistically, humourously. On the rug. Sitting cross-legged. Hirsute Buddhas. They take deep breaths of polluted city air. Feel good anyway. O.R. smiles. Dominique keeps on watching her without a single muscle movement in his face. Frozen, immobile. A happy corpse. O.R. bounces around, tries every way of distracting him. Dances around him. The gleaming and tinkling of dimestore jewellery. With one hand Dominique makes O.R. lie down beside him. Why his violence? Because it's in the rules of an old game.

42

Still in the month of July. O.R., Dominique and Mathieu are visiting. The cemetery. Flowers at the foot of the graves. Tombstones. Names. Words written to show regret.

They see things but don't think them. Death is somewhere else. Their presence in this green place, named Côte des Neiges Cemetery. Words.

## 43

The words take place. On a surface. In a precise time. An atmosphere. They represent the main characters, mask reality … and little by little the mask becomes the reality. The only reality, created in the book in one's hand, a reality-atmosphere we will buy at any price when it comes time to forget a little.

*The consumed words*

The words' value: $2.00 per page or more depending on the demand. Monied words. Wealth. Like all wealth, reassuring.

A CHART OF SEVERAL WORDS

| | | |
|---|---|---|
| quiet revolution | 1962 | liberals |
| dialogue | 1965 | catholics |
| progressive conservative | 1969 | conservatives |
| corporate commando | 1969 | union nationale |
| silent majority | 1969 | republicans |
| galloping revolution | 1970 | union nationale |

Standing beneath the price charts, Dominique C. makes a few notes before going back to work.

## 44

Easy words. Words which come and take their place on the page in the chance stream of thoughts.
or
rare words
plentiful words but well organized
or
superfluous words.

45

Dominique, Mathieu and Henri at the tavern. Sitting at the back of the room. For the pleasure of having a cheap drink in company. The noise of chairs, curses, the Expos at bat.
Problematical words.
Henri powerless at playing with words today. To recover the exact meaning of the group's words or forget once and for all. But. Dominique and Mathieu confused, uneasy. The male variables around them, blowing their noses, spitting, smiling. Mathieu: Jeze I don't feel so good.

## 46

A sunny bedroom. O.R. sitting at her work table. Hunched over a book of pictures and words, stories and letters. Her hand on the paper. Her hand, fingers. The image in relief. A small sculpture under the fingers. Soft, round, fragile. Now O.R. is looking out the window. A sunny street. Dominique crossing the street, his arms filled with groceries. This in the morning.

But in the evening. O.R.'s elbows leaning on the work table. The bedroom dimly lit. The picture book open on the table. O.R.'s silhouette on the badly lit wall.

O.R. with the book, dozing.

47

And so this page. Because the text wants to focus upon itself: the characters disappear, the words empty of their meaning little by little. Thus the text: a deluxe (lifeless) object. Superfluous.

The text here: an easy target. The text revealed, explaining and demonstrating its construction. To everyone. The text demystified. Not the text for much longer, unless thought of differently in its elucidation, its use.

Dominique C. in the Stock Exchange building. With two secretaries who work with her. Dominique C. isolated in her stubborn silence. Problematical words.

48

O.R. kneeling on a chair, near the window. Rain. The pane steamy. O.R. tracing letters. Clever fingers. On a smooth glass surface. Dominique C. sitting at the opposite end of the room. Holding a glass of milk. Mathieu who has just arrived and who is talking softly of the rain today and the beautiful weather yesterday. Time passes slowly.

O.R. at the window, wiping it with the back of her hand. Their strange passivity at this hour when the whole city is swarming. Their pleasure, their joy in the silence, the half-dark of the gray day.

Throughout the text, the book, the same characters, same names, same development.

Dominique C. holding an empty glass.

## 49

Clarification. Indispensable in this long circumstance we call a book.

1. Experiencing words: living for a while in their wake.
2. Experiencing characters: marginal.
3. Situation: discontinuous. Ellipsis and montage. A staged situation.
4. Clarification: form in the form. An interruption which only adds to the discontinuity in the event.

Clarification. More or less indispensable now that the text meets its reality as text.

## 50

All five of the variables parading along under the street lights and neon signs. Placards above their heads, shouts, slogans. The sound of motorcycles, sirens. A molotov cocktail or two. A scuffle. A riot, as they're sometimes called.

O.R., Dominique, Henri, Mathieu and Dominique C. together again after two hours of wandering among people looking for and finding each other. Exhausted.

The words surface again: numerous and useless. The night ends in impotence, in conversation.

## 51

Between the pages: a mode of thought which can bring about a synthesis of active desire with passive joy. Source of this attentive quest of knowledge.

Through the characters and by way of the text.

O.R. summed up in a few gestures, two or three words. Her attitude in the book: the attitude required for reading.

O.R. or Dominique or Henri or Mathieu or Dominique C. One and the same character, the definitive image of a young community softly approaching the very core of a wholly marginal reality.

Dominique sitting on the steps of the stairway. In front of the house. A few passersby in the shade. Still this crushing heat which weighs upon even the most pleasant activities. Dominique and the city. A flower in the asphalt jungle, as they say. But Dominique, in spite of appearances, at this precise hour of the evening, in his jeans and T-shirt, on a different wavelength than the one produced by the asphalt jungle, the dirty stinking back lanes, as they say.
Dominique sitting in a cliché, in a setting so well described elsewhere. Dominique in a scandalous position. To understand: Dominique sitting on the edge of the pool. His legs in the water. Flowers in the garden. Red and lovely and yellow also. Dominique in the shade happily waiting for O.R. to come back.
Especially to understand: Dominique being used as propaganda tool for the sadness of streets without horizons, for the right to live, for the revolution.

53

In terms of awareness, Dominique and O.R. and the others illustrate one means. In the text, they help make the words advance on a surface. They postulate both doubt and certainty.
The text more elliptical than ever.
Ellipsis upon ellipsis, the text accumulates the delays.
Incoherence is still to be anticipated.
During this time O.R. is making a meal. Knife in one hand, onion in the other. Time passes. Supper time. The hour devoted to food. The pleasures of the table, as they say.

54

The importance given the birth, the existence of a book! Fiction outstrips reality. No. But reality is always lived to the extent that fiction allows the real to be embodied in the mind. Strange process, strange progress.
To come back to life after having verified life in a book. (!).
Between the possible and the impossible, the text and the characters: creation. A thin margin of safety between reality and the wish for another reality. O.R., Dominique and the others in a space defined by their own limits: they are what they are and have no wish to be otherwise. They use themselves to the limit. The very reason for their silence among the variables.

55

Henri and Dominique on the tennis court. Bright sunshine. Balls bouncing, soaring, bouncing back. A white ball. A fuzzy ball in the palm of the hand. A bad serve. The small black pang of the loser. Actions, spent energy. Their hands trembling. A dull noise in their heads. Rubbery legs. Dominique and Henri stretched out on the lawn. In the green. Children's voices. A mad dog running in all directions. Time passes.

56

O.R., Mathieu and Dominique C. busy making supper. Tidying up every room in the house.
Shower. Rest.
Dominique and Henri back again. Shower. Nap. Eight o'clock. O.R. the first up. Time to share the meal.
All through the night: sensations not felt in words.

## 57

Night, this night. A night of pleasure and fantasy. In the yellow light. In the large room leading to the balcony.
The lighting changes with each hour, the possibilities with each word. A new approach with each movement, every wish.
The characters blend and fade into each other in the diffuse light. The night is lived in slow motion. In silence.
Variable.
Night. All five sitting around the table. Footsteps on the cement outside. Inside, the shadows and bodies of Dominique, O.R., Mathieu, Henri, Dominique C. The shadows of five characters with names. Recoverable by reading the text which describes them in the night, in the obsessive light of the big room leading to the balcony.

## 58

Henri and Mathieu at Dominique C.'s place. In a green area. Bent over some vegetable plants. Dominique C. in the clear water of the swimming pool. The sun. Colours of things and bodies. The smell of suntan lotion. At the edge of the pool, white paper and princely grass. Dominique C. happy, a fish in the water. Henri and Mathieu still stooped over the same tomato plants. Discussing the nutritional value of these tomatoes planted by the fine slim hands of Dominique C.'s *aggressive old man*.

## 59

Some time yet before the text obliterates everything about the characters and their attitudes. Still a few pages before O.R. and Dominique start to work, to EARN THEIR LIVING. A few words before the words leave the story suspended.
O.R. and Dominique. Hand in hand. In the crowd, variables. Looking upward. The first burst of fireworks. A white trail of long spermatozoa wiggling in the black sky. The sparkles slowly dying. The slow fall of artificial fire. The variables finally shoulder to shoulder in a holiday atmosphere. The crowd. Popcorn. Policeman: every holiday in Quebec being a holiday of losers.
O.R. and Dominique with noses in the air under the fireworks nose-diving in their direction. The hour is over. The variables leave slowly, humbly.

## 60

Still some time left
before they all go out to EARN THEIR LIVING, before the words weave an opaque tissue of literature over their lives, their freedom, so that together we can once more see 'several attitudes which happen to have been noticed in the past few hours.'[1]

[1] Nicole Brossard, trans. Larry Shouldice, *A Book,* in *The Blue Books* (Toronto: Coach House Books, 2003; original edition Montréal: Editions du jour, 1970; first English edition Toronto: Coach House Press, 1976), page 17.

## 61

Textual analysis: through the text and the spaces. Everything is to be taken up again and followed through to the present. O.R. and Dominique's past. Their former life. The event is liable to destroy completely the carefully created atmosphere sustained from figure 1 to number five. O.R. and Dominique whose opinions remain marginal in this text that pushes logic to the point of wanting completely to recover their availability.
This text which can still only affirm that description or narration do not generally manage to create anything other than another thing.
O.R. and Dominique in the restaurant. Between noon and one o'clock. Between the time to leave and the time to go back. Time passes. Differently. Quickly.

## 62

For the crowd quickly becomes a specific place. A hard and impenetrable thing which words are not able to dissociate from its five letters.

O.R. and Dominique at five o'clock. Towards the métro. In the rain. The crowd compact. Crushing. The smell of wet clothes. Dominique looking uneasy (only uneasy).

The crowd.

63

The banalities of time are apparent throughout this look at the past. Those of the text, in this story about words which are continually taking on importance. O.R. and Dominique are waiting. The coffee is getting cold. O.R. is impatient, with other things to do but wait for friends who don't come when they are supposed to. The sugar in the bottom of the cup. The bill. Time to leave. O.R. and Dominique have no time left. Life takes place in the future. In the hope of gaining time, earning their living.

64

A definite parenthesis.
O.R. and Dominique after lovemaking, lying against one another on the rumpled bed. Words superfluous. Silence. The characters in the text. Assimilated into this long analysis which is not the one the manuscript suggested. An analysis whose success or failure in each sentence depends on the one preceding or following it.
Later, in the middle of the night, O.R. sitting at her work table. A book of pictures in front of her. Her shadow strange in Dominique's eyes as he half opens them. Time. O.R. with the book closed. Her shadow. The bedroom. Mattress noises. O.R. and Dominique in the margin of night.

## 65

The living room. The heat unbearable. O.R. naked. From the living room to the balcony. Naked. O.R.'s body chosen and described in terms of a cultural convention: O.R. beautiful → O.R. naked → O.R. free → O.R. and the scandal of freedom. See page 24. Her explanation above. Later, the five o'clock crowd. O.R. and Dominique at the entrance of the CIL building, on Dorchester Boulevard, between the cars. Precipitated into a mad race towards a parked bus. Which pulls away at that very moment. At the moment when the ink traces a path between the rough pores of the paper. Then dries. Thus.

66

Time precious and happy. Prior to these pages of explanation which reintroduce previous characters and which also allow O.R. and Dominique to remain characters. Still. This time in a restrictive setting. Through words acceded to and accepted but which always tend to flee whatever is real: someone *writing* a life.

## 67

Step by step. The words follow one another through the variables. Are repeated according to certain obligations which rather resemble a wish to push previous attempts still further. Thus the cycle of variables varies very little in spite of the new impression that emerges each time the manuscript gradually becomes the book.
O.R., Dominique and Mathieu sitting on the porch in front of the house. Tired out from their day.
The variables parade before their eyes / they become fixed in the looks of others.

68

O.R. sitting in the rest room. Green walls. The space between the green: carpeted. A box of Kleenex on the table comer. A tube of lipstick. O.R. eats her sandwich. With the employees. Feeling foreign to the words being spoken around her. Also to those who use her initials and abuse them over and over again, to the extent that this someone who is choosing wants to.
O.R.: initials.

69

O.R.: initials. Letters at the start of a name no one has yet spoken.
O.R. which through repetition has become a word in itself, a word which first suggests the colour of gold and then *or*, the conjunction 'now' used to join and connect certain names and to allow for transitions between the characters.
O.R. remain initials, but manage to coincide with O.R. in her role as character, in everyday life, that is between four and five o'clock, some time yet before the offices close.

70

Between the eye and the printed page: the distance between the thumb and the index finger: a book held between two hands: reading. O.R., holding a book. Leaning against a tree. In the middle of the park. Her eyes looking skyward. Under the foliage of some tree or other.

Why, under the tree, O.R., do reading and this imminent distance seem like another piece of reading, a different beginning?

71

Time.
Reading being done.
Take time: follow the rhythm, the spell.
What spell?
In the magic that comes completely from within, in the chest cavity and the other: the magic of everyday gestures: seeing and touching.
Whence reading.
The words take on meaning behind the eyelids. The reading looks like this, that, the other, like this reading which already depends on the preceding one.

72

A page in which the tree and O.R. look more like stylized figures being read and touched according to their respective degrees of availability.
The tree in no way symbolic, with O.R. sliding her fingernails along its bark, somehow scratching out stylized figures which look more like printed letters than like the leaves O.R. is trying desperately to have appear on the very trunk of the tree.
Beneath the leaves.

## 73

And now, supposing for the time being that the characters give way to those other characters who come and go in the book, from one page to another, from one glimpse to another. Supposing that O.R. also becomes a reader and is no longer hidden in the guise of a character. O.R. with the page before her, diligently confronting the words as if she herself held the pen that indefinitely lengthens the sentences and arranges them in different perspectives each time the flesh conceives of its pleasure and thus formulates it, with the result that, all around, things remain suspended.

## 74

O.R. is reading about her character, beside Dominique. Surrounded by Mathieu, Henri and Dominique C. In the kitchen, as before, as described in the first pages of this book. O.R. with her character, who is sitting on a wooden chair in the yellow light. Open and smiling in this tepid night which is as pleasurable as the bodies of those who sit facing the character and each another, sharing the passing hours.

O.R.: the distance separating her initials from her character, her character from herself. O.R. the reader.

75

O.R. and sight. This in the tradition according to which all knowledge and pleasure are founded in sight. This also because the eye is a meeting. A vital centre circle from which all desire emanates, to which primary intentions return in various forms. O.R., looking wide-eyed at a shop window, its reflection, on Sainte-Catherine Street. After work.

## 76

Dominique and Mathieu in the corner Snack Bar. Late in the evening. The same customers as yesterday and the day before yesterday. The waitress. Her new hairdo. Dishes clattering on the counter. The explosion of a fifteenth bomb is reported on the radio. Dominique and Mathieu in the text after the explosion: only characters.

O.R., her eyes glued to the text (this one) which situates her outside the event: spectator and reader.

77

Oui et non. Amour et paix. Yes or no. Love and peace. On page 93 it is difficult for words and things to do without commentary. Oui ou non: agree or refuse: forget versus act. Words thrown confusedly into the fabric of the event: O.R. and Dominique C. at Place Ville-Marie, surrounded. Air conditioning. Snatches of English words, snatches of conversations in English and other languages, tout autour. O.R. and Dominique C. Their words: more like murmurs.

78

The variables passing by. Dominique at the window. Rain falling. The sky is gray and peaceful. The bedroom quiet. Dominique is alone and happy. Time goes on, but slowly.

The words take life elsewhere.

The certitude that every pore, muscle, every particle is fulfilling its function. A happy body. Living. Its shadow barely noticeable in the setting. The realism of the setting. This bedroom in which Dominique acknowledges inside himself that life is life, that only a tautology can connect the two extremities. But the book demands more and less for it describes what is beneath and beyond life – and joy, forgetfulness make it superficial, though precious.

79

Another page and on this page the words that O.R. and Mathieu are trying to forget. Words read in the morning newspaper. O.R. and Mathieu during their coffee break: why are they so vulnerable? Now that.

80

O.R. sitting at her work table, writing an anonymous letter to the newspaper. Remaining anonymous: being the person who writes on behalf of others. But O.R. puts the words in such a way that the whole letter is only a speech about anonymous letters, about anonymous texts published in letter form, that are left at the entrances of buildings. Anonymous letters, F.L. and others, abbreviations. An anonymous text incomprehensible to the old grammar.
A neutral text because politically committed texts would be signed.
On the table, the ink bottle, the pen, the empty sheets of paper, the others, covered with simple words O.R. offers to the reader with the fear that he will read them without countersigning them.
*He lowers his head and agrees. His gesture is anonymous.*

81

The softness, slowness of their movements. O.R., Dominique and Dominique C.: love in a threesome. Everything about their looks, their hesitation, their actions contributes to the heightening of desire. They open up with pleasure. A unity regained and … lost as soon as memory recalls the time of this unity.

## 82

On page 98, Henri, his character, the man and the image.
Henri leaning on a pinball machine. In old man Lejeune's old restaurant. A player. Henri moves aside. Little silver balls. The noise of dingers and buzzers. Colour, colours. The racket. Players, coffee-drinkers, smokers, idlers, being listed.
Henri a few minutes before going back to work. At the end of page 98. Every bit as tense as the someone who is turning the page.

83

Everyone together at Dominique C.'s place. Watching television. To hear the election results. Figures, votes, men, names of ridings, letters. Predictions and interviews. Analyses. Faces. Grand schemes. Nervousness most of all.
The winners.
Grand words. Shouts. The racket.
'This is a great day for Québec. I am very happy. We shall do everything in our power to work for the good of Québec.'
Two o'clock in the morning. Dominique C.'s father offers his daughter and the others a drink. The evening is over. Dominique C.'s father is left alone. Standing in his living room. Holding a glass of whiskey.

84

Silence: O.R. leaning against Dominique's shoulder.

85

The words. An atmosphere. The lives of a few individuals: the characters in this book, the pages in this book, rather ordinary but complete unto themselves, ordinary but.

O.R. and Dominique. Their working hours in the CIL building. To distrust problematical words, problematical life. From up on the twentieth storey: the city. Montréal. Montréal. Ville-Marie. Hochelaga. The words circle above the city. Victim.

86

O.R. and Dominique sitting eating cold leftover chicken. Lovers: smiles. O.R.'s (Dominique's) hands on Dominique's (O.R.'s) cheeks, forehead, lips.

The text

and several variables

Words looking for other words. To be inserted in the spaces that from the beginning were considered the key elements of this book.

And the spaces?

## 87

Things happen. 'Everything happens.' The book and the story of its characteristics, its composition. Life makes continual adjustments to the orders coming from outside, to inner necessities. Also. Everything is accomplished within the logic of passing time which nothing can stop.
The book in this same perspective.

88

O.R. sitting in the bath. Hot water. Soap bubbles. Her thighs: the wet shining skin. O.R. bathing in soapy water, as if in her blood. Sensual. Dominique sitting on the floor, beside the bathtub. Holding a book. Reading. O.R. listens while rubbing Steinberg's pink soap over her skin. The words come. Dissolved in the babble of the water splashing about in the tub. Word-waves (cf. Roland Giguère). To be discussed: the ownership of the text. Originality: being the first or the second?

## 89

After eighty-nine pages of text, the words resurface again. Slowly, according to schedule. According to the chronometer of this someone who plans the culmination of the book in about ten pages.
Because two hundred or three hundred or five hundred pages would not change the first hundred sheets of this manuscript,
or rather
because it still remains to be proven that a manuscript should have 125 to 150 or 198 pages to gain the status of a book.
Words: O.R. and the others hunched laboriously over their work tables. Between two and three o'clock in the afternoon.

## 90

The characters together for the last time in the text. In an American restaurant on Saint-Hubert Street. Variables all around. O.R., Dominique and Mathieu, Dominique C. and Henri. Leaning their elbows on the brown arborite. Reading the menu. O.R.: to remain free and at the mercy of no one. Henri: you think so?
In the text
the characters file past the cash register. A single bill: \$8.00. Outside, it is still sunny. O.R. and Dominique take the métro.

## 91

To be aware of what happens at the very instant the eyes focus on the hand holding the book, on the book and the words it is made up of. From a distance. As the reading is done, the change occurs. Second by second the character is abstracted from her character. O.R. conceived by herself as one more person, being transformed along with the others. Dominique looks at her and doesn't remember a thing. Guesses what she's like from a distance: one young woman with the others. Himself a multiple character in this space where men, women and others disappear in the multitude.

## 92

Mathieu out of breath, jostled by the variables. At the corner of Peel and Sainte-Catherine. Astounded by the force of this enormous thing pushing him along. A little further each time. And finally forcing him to change direction. To follow the course of things, like the following text: keep going even if it means a complete change dependent upon the sway of this thing which keeps inviting one to turn back.

To suppress the rest.

93

But the rest remains a thing to be written. A few more words – in spite of the reduced vocabulary – always the same ones, repeated in a different context.

These few more words: O.R. and Dominique more and more aware of their beauty. Tuned in to the *scenes* of horror happening around them.

94

O.R., a tiny dot in the light of a street lamp. In the night. Waiting. An image (in the text) of O.R. leaning against the long stem of the street lamp. Tiny in the dark.

Or

this variable who sets up the contrast between O.R. (character) leaning against a metal pole and O.R. backed against this same pole with her eyes staring in front of her.

The text and its attempts:

something more in O.R.'s eyes. Late in the night.

95

Rain. Dawn. Life comes to the fore again. Henri has just paid the money for his release on bail.

The city is gray and beautiful: a question of atmosphere more than anything. Of presence also.

Henri in his head the night of the interrogation. In the bus the variables are silent.

Henri, his arrest, the pain in the back of his neck. Around him the variables are stirring. Coming and going on this Monday morning in September.

96

The manuscript: someone bends over blank paper and calmly composes the very reason for his inclination to. The page, reduced to the characters' dimensions: setting. Does or doesn't the manuscript isolate the five beings who move around within the closed space of its body – its interior.

97

The event moves toward its close.
O.R. and Dominique facing Henri. Silence. An intuition, a certainty that for someone in the future life and death hold something more than merely a controlled impatience with problematical words.
The route is in no way changed. From now on it is understood.
The text and the spaces.
For the words cannot sum up everything for you: O.R., Dominique, Mathieu, Dominique C., Henri, you, the others.

98

The words are yours.

## 99

The game is over. The book too. The manuscript is no more. O.R., Dominique, Mathieu, Dominique C. and Henri continue on. Time passes slowly, so slowly. Someone is reading. And gently closes the object.

# Turn of a Pang

by Nicole Brossard
traduced by Patricia Claxton

*Turn of a Pang* is a translation of *Sold-out (étreinte–illustration)*, which was first published in 1973 by Editions du Jour.



This translation was first published as *Turn of a Pang* in 1976 by Coach House Press as part of the Quebec Translations series, edited by Barbara Godard and Frank Davey.

Things that HIT YOU IN THE EYE with a view to modifying unconnected clues mobile motives – toward 'latent complicities' change of attitudes then wonderment.

But the redhead was only the redhead and thence came the difficulty of living the redhead to the full hiding under that head of hair, that sumptuous arrogant mane.

The hidden side.

Radio noises rain down thick in the little kitchen. The tapwater runs a bit too hot not hot enough. The day-to-day gets short shrift in the anonymous adult head bent over the sink, curious and hirsute like a plump fruit hanging over a wall.

The redhead, stepped over carefully in the shag-rugged living room, the redhead at rest, reclining sleeping living stone slowly breathing human stone in that red living room space its occupants some twenty men and women and a few children furtive images of adult faces bathed at this point in sweat smooth water streaming from foreheads from temples down to round soft downy chins in this living room whose atmosphere might recall others but which one remembers most returning to a midsummer quebec night's dream dimly lit and rather erotic when magical thoughts triumphed over those verbal battles busily waged by adults in the adult world here and there time and again in supermarkets ministries and elsewhere too.

The redhead, stepped over carefully …

Just before, or immediately <u>in</u> the second at hand, a fleeting personal adventure far on the horizon, in the lines of the hand escape and tenderness as in a supreme interpretation of life and death; coming close to past images in a story that wasn't one but in which once deep inside we might expect to find the most transparent clarity

or immediately (sounds of ice in glasses)

Realization of cold in the room the twin of the one next door only a different colour in which a water bed was never anything but a water bed. Stupidly to sleep on.

(ice in glasses)

As for the evening's final words, they mingle strategically with the all-pervading smoke (swallowed held lovingly in the throat).

As regards the redhead, there's only the colour in the glint in my eye in the brightness of my smile cunningly arranging sexes and lips around the silhouettes the time wouldn't survive the excitement would it and

Yes I was dropping softly nicely down

Well traced drawn the line: fingers idly on the dusty glass-topped table in the hall wandering glances right and left, caresses to the cheek another of the major's last goodnights. Balancing over the glass patiently awaiting the distant mirage miracle eyes approaching eyes in the wavy light reflections from the polished surface. Four times the same little wave of the hand and nod of goodbye.

An idea that a redhead (or rusty red the colour of her hair) might be the profile and surface of the story of a text taking us back to the days of wide high heels, of a fashion undebauched except by the wind blowing from behind the Notre Dame Street armament plants. An idea of resemblance with early conscription text that darts here and there weaves the under side of a double-ended reality '41–'71 (a trail of invisible Ariadne thread leading from one century to another in thirty years of life and privacy in collective isolation in a territory waiting for renewed loves and friendships, backslaps, passionate caresses coursing paroxysms seizing petrified spines of (hunted) wartime lovers, when she wore black (in mourning for her father) svelte and radiant to be hanging on his arm, his young mistress. He (as the picture shows) walks in such a way as to advance gently.

The days of picture postcards in glossy colour, days of cards in pale pastels arriving from Old Orchard. Look closely at this common ground where the romantic come and go of those days perpetuates through the thirty years or thereabouts separating 'forty-one and nowadays age of biological maturity, orgasm full, fleeting and total in the radiant conscious human animal (quite beyond words but integral in the writing filling space / meandering calligraphy mask of all conceived and stirring in that still firm and tender flesh).

And on the back behind the pink and blue and sea-splash silvery spittle between the rocks, a three-cent stamp the face of Lincoln cancelled.

a) red, rust: adj. and n.
'And the little toy soldier is
red with rust' (Eugene Field)
'She has the charming mien of
an adorable redhead' (Apollinaire)
'Her hair warm and red
as burnt gold' (Villiers)

It stuck (DNA) and one day
reappeared quite unsought in
what the tapping typewriter wrote.

Provocative hue.

Hazy image of that redhead woman reclining on the rug. Not much to note save the all-important colour. Recollection or imagination taking pleasure in reversing the chronological order of events delight in the chase and knowing how it is for my generation born in those times and was for men and women who saw them born. This is not written from memory. Here no personal experience of life as it was in those conscription days. How things looked, shades of rouge and lipstick, the price of cigarettes, the smell of factory smoke, the taste of pale ale, all this is history and comes from books.

Avid stare. Falling snow. Mild fluctuating weather. The line of trees bare fingers clutching at the gray today. Gusting buffeting suddenly the wind but inside you listen and you try with writing to bring forth silhouettes of strange (mythical) specimens of men who come on horseback in bands and leave traces and clues for the eye to grasp … like an image spreading on the screen when a *Winchester* goes off.

Burst of fine snow blown against the window panes.

And then slipping in with time's passage as wind gusting through cracks between boards comes the moment of truth when man confronts man each to destroy the other. When on the screen closeup comes the man's hat and strains of music yet unheard reach the ear from near from far.

A parody of snow on memory's window pane.

The searching eye.

Eye roving moist glistening system for interpreting the reality in the game of words, complicity of hand and eye induced by the nineteen forties' red mane and wig

(here near the Main in a nightclub not far from the well-known whorehouse at Amherst and Ontario, wigged blondes and redheads preen for watching eyes in the blur)

red / dyed swirling about itself

The transparency in things opposed to verbal clutter; growing white dot surrounded with rusty red the white spreading lavish covering the red (which fades by degrees as a colour become an obsessional presence / link / all of which belongs already like snow to nostalgia that never drains its source of meaning.

Eye and memory out to lampoon the colour rusty red.

View from across the street. A tram goes by on Bélanger Street. Children wearing great red wax lips. Raspberry flavour. Slow pace of the past cancelling out the effect of anything said that's new and centred on the joy of life. A past relived (so little) imagined with care and philosophic need to understand and want (with a logic other than the logic of those days) the blandishing reality.

An image and at once allusion to that pair of lips locked in wax, whence the silence or (the child's incoherent muttering behind the little crimson mask). Words contained in a game that's worth the candle … in certain eyes …

Then there's the memory of after-post-war days (fragmented memory).

Prospects (from palm lines to forehead lines and a few skin folds on a smooth stomach); but then reading the future would make no difference because the terrible lines of fate are hardly drawn in rusty red like a trademark to be <u>read</u> and pronounced properly P E N C I L O knowing beforehand that what's written is offered without guarantee.

Tried oh so hard to reproduce a set of tarots the castles Gleason used to make with cards and that red (briefly visible in the blue geography of the king's jester's habit)

and also the Emerald Tablet whose text he'd retranscribed on China paper or with India ink retraced the golden age of 'that which is above is like to that which is below.'

The redhead seated by his side fine shadows of her hair on the white wall behind. The wax drips (blow the flame black) the light goes out someone IN A CRASH OF GLASS THE CANDLE.

A face with long beard bristling. The ragman sandman in person passing by along the street never does anything worse. July '43 on Garnier Street, crickets chirp. Hoards of children suffocate in the heat (it must be noon) and that one there's an anecdote on all those moving lips, on Garnier Street while a band goes by, coloured form resounding in the wobbly midday air.

An anecdote in the eye.

## CHAPTER ONE

Flashback (countdown of years to October 1941 ——— ——— Citizen Kane / Loew's 'THE SENSATION OF A NATION' seen and reread behind a memory screen a poster stuck [all those tongues just think] on the movie house wall announcing magically how the verb devour could devour to satiation so much attentive flesh (its surrender when it happens mirror fashion to arouse those gargantuan appetites that a roomful of enthralled spectators in suspension always satisfies).

At every moment (in the queue the spinning) you'd have to expect to see ahead (spidery plot in hot censored climate as lips part looking more and more like vulva to be coloured [wax crayon and contour] as in the image-language children use for secret passages and obsidian lamps) a description of a place and men in broad-brimmed hats and painted ties, feminine mechanisms and procedures said to be oriental once the lipstick colour decoded (recollecting also the scent wafting from the whole mouth whole apple a gleeful comparison [like in a surplus of material]).

Citizen Kane and the same night the El Morocco opening on Mansfield Street 'leading me astray in so many stages on the stools red and resistant to alcohol white and brown, meandering beers and blonde tufts multiplied in my beard oh cunnilingus' the opening and gaping of the El Morocco, the 'oath' circulating among the customers – sharpies and soldiers – under the table nylon frays and bags – curves a word occurring in the time to cross legs ——— cross of thighs under long dress suggesting modesty (Cherry would show up and smile) belatedly indeed for that's done it sweet consuming contact lingering lost in fleshly depths cruel respectful caressing lashes.

Regular perched at the Bar after work. PHOTO, and below the caption, 'Women at work applying airplane fabric … ' Another one, red on her lips, gone on her clientèle, factory rhythmics first on her mind. Weary regular clocked, ready to pass out; heat and mechanics of the gift of life down the drain in wear and tear to the sound of ringing metal and the touch of harsh fabric made for combat of unknown bodies no less eager than the bodies of customers sweating out the dancefloor and torrid October.

Bright-eyed regular conversing the current conversation which means chit-chat about luxuries and when-the-war's-over. Hear the jingle of blackened pennies teeming in drawers which keep away the verdigris from the ennobled face of George VI who struck in copper is a greater threat to peace of mind and body than the censored NEWS at the Granada.

All the streetlamps in the blue-black evenings of July were yellow moons like round moon faces.

Visible (written thus: the body becomes visible through the power of imagery and desire) <u>vivid river moulded in ink</u> (flow as in fauna and flora fl).

Together simultaneously the sense of seeing the visible become an abstraction 'the strangest position in which a mortal could find himself.'

Point of departure inscribed as such in the double play of writing and d-death as *lived* at times of great lucidity, as *prolonged* in the night (sometimes in the afternoon come siesta and solitude) to the sound of heavy trucks passing far away (not very far) while with wide-open eyes one listens to one's palpitating heart, legs apart or together crossed.

The trace      the multiplicity of movements in that time remembered for the ease with which certain caresses grew from the scalp, neck or hip. The preciseness of the moment; the thrust of haunches forcing breath, cutting short its sounds, turning them to enchanted havoc under red-tinted flesh that SHATTERING pulverizing instant.

The single trace in the iris (cat's eye) surprise cleft … the stomach asserts its presence on the page and to the eye is always magnified by the round-about approach.

A bit of everything in this trumped-up tale of childhood and maturity. Whatever opens the door for acquaintance with times past rich with experience and awareness put to the test by writing that exploits it and compels it to take form.

In rusty red or elsewhere, near factories in Montréal. PRODUCTION.

The formative act that is the sense metamorphosed / metamorphosing (the red of the wig over the black of the pale-face woman's hair).

A trumped-up tale with varied reflections in avalanche (presuming snow) and multiple effects according to the points of view.
The instant.
Terrain conducive to dispersion, wandering and rearrangement word for word, for counterbalance precisely as in the word *grace*: 'he with plumed and high-crowned hat who never bears arms but yields them to all comers paler purer white than what's left of the page.'

Encounters seen obliquely or the outline of bodies perceived in the proper way; attracting to oneself the opponent's eye (even using the other's resistance the better to arouse desire) insinuating by that the risk of seeing hazy forms in movement, from that far removed in mirages that are beautiful or cloud one's vision with the extreme terror they inspire

which amplifies everything and deeply disturbs pores and muscles and mind frenzied by encounters seen obliquely.

The anecdote ramifies following recollection's course in the protraction of colours and forms returning to the eye some years later. And in the telling it draws from time past only the fictional necessities. Tells of a presence in an uncertain city (how the expectations lived in it augur the remorse of having lived ridiculously and in the fleeting and also fictional reality of it all at that) passionately the many hours of desire and its dispersion.

Problematics of the colour rusty red reproduced endlessly in red-dyed hair throughout the years (or rather the streets, their historic British names of victory and defeat, their French names from overseas) imitation of excellence, imitation period blustering into place in fictional tongue.

Anecdotic but as briefly as can be in fashioning the event.

The setting and its honourable mentions (Laurentian and Gaspesian zones) in phony storybook development. Rolled virgin parchment of text which exists only for the endless imperative search. An enchanted thought on the occasional occasion of a quebec night beneath the ceiling of pyrotechnics and untwinkling stars.

Fiction admitted to the inner sanctum of symbolic warmth.

The rusty red of bodies male and / or female. Funny how now the text dilutes and is lost in the scarification that adorns an author's stomach. If all hands could touch his stomach together they would read ..........................................................................................
....................................................................................................
....................................................................................................
skin et cætera.

Rusty red / reality: Belmont Park its monstrous folksy dolls laughing their mechanical laugh fit to kill.

Conquest over thought, conquest over yesterday's torment and today's in surges of credulity, and long waits.

Manifestations of intense reflection; signed, delivered (smile) or deep black imagined trace soot signs sequence sz.

Drawer.

Closed: the year 'forty-one, no more barbarous than another, closed again with arms and thighs closed around slim adult bodies silhouettes sculptures. Fiction-actuality of painted lips (Baby we'll paint the town t'night). Lips and thighs open in that little green and gray Ontario Street bedroom. Little panties on the floor, on the devarnished varnish, lacy garter belt (Je vois la vie en rose).

Irresistible urge to sleep and dream (moist cotton-wool sex) vague vagary of a song sung high beneath the weeping willow, foliage above m-me (from that day on she had herself called Cherry).

Cherry dreaming in the rusty red of iodized cotton wool. She worked in Dupuis Frères' basement, in children's underwear. She'd scratched her finger on a rusty nail.

Irresistible urge to waken? Interrogation: tomorrow or tomorrow Sunday or Sunday in three weeks?

*Rubis sur l'ongle*: pronto, ruby red of fingernail: Cherry.

EVA / APRIL: thirty-year-old cheesecake pinup whose young body whose yellowed paper remind me of nothing important at all.

Dorchester Boulevard to cross. The time of day when rusty red looks (diffused in the glass of high wide windows) vaguely like a sunset.

*Trèfle incarnat* their perfume, powdered lipsticked red and white dark-haired daughters of respectable families passing through the revolving doors of the Sun Life the tallest building of all. Nineteen hundred and forty-one in the hand of secretaries employees experts in the fabrication of sumptuous letters opulent in the long sweep of their f's and g's successive curlicues magnificent f's.

SCRIBES

A quebec night (recalled pigheadedly as such to make all seem cheerful almost true by dint of incantation) lived beneath the sky and the chinese red neon lights of Old Montréal. Warm malleable night, plastic as braggadocio would have it. Lurid with luring letters. Circumscribed, hallucinogenic, rhythmed night of soft docile substance on which to lie and not to dream of a world, dense nocturnal halo around the centre of attraction where dying would be other than by chance.

The tourist homes beckon through the dark of this same night. A world apart this quadrilateral [Sainte-Catherine – Saint-Paul / Saint-Laurent – Saint-Denis] ! Festivity or conspiracy, a tourist home's just the thing. Room rented for the evening or the night, handily out of reach of the police, finding oneself among friends, talking, smoking, awash with music and rusty red, shadowed jostled by profiles on the white of walls, rooted on the cold oak floor.

Purlieu, tense sequences on display in the Leduc Pharmacy window (twenty-four hours a day / day and night). HArbour, CHerrier, LAfontaine, WAlnut, telephone exchanges knit into one's memory as a single reality. To be dialed to reach a friend when you need one, someone, some stormy night when white spills white, slowly for hours on end.

Snow and sonic background of *Echoes / Meddle /* nighttime harmony and more, the ink trajectory, for without that image of sequence and silk, the harmony would seem too uselessly like some figure from the past.

Nineteen hundred and seventy-one an evening in May, pinpointed in time Montréal space and its smell; nineteen hundred and forty-one: baby crying behind the bars of his playpen flowered rubber garden. The world begins with the bursting of shells (oh please not his playpen!). The fabled fictitious quebec night has just begun drags on like waiting in a station.

Drawer.

A network of equivalences to be conquered following the thread of each allusion, each textual membrane (transparent / opaque) formation, disappearance.

'41–'71 in the rusty red all around the faces that one sees palpable unreasoningly.

A crowd, anonymity. Splendid back ahead, flowing hair; curve of hips or lines of hip moving in tune with that back, be it man or woman, a network of beckoning indicators. To be followed step by step breathing down his / her neck through the labyrinth of English Montréal *how I'd like to follow someone else somewhere else on the black side of this island. The black wave of I happily rendering to pleasure* my French everyday logic stymied, possible sources of fulfillment too.

"I'm coming"
Of everything said that evening, by this extract understand that the summary of yesterday and today (lifelong presence, courage always wanting; thus, with the touch of round clear groomed fingernails 'I'm coming, yes, yes' derisive gaze in the mirror, after, seeing the effect of that liquid between those legs) predicts the effect

or rather the sensation it brings lingering in the nerve centres and other centres of life and pain and tenderness or joy as in that trace still fresh in the mind's eye drawn by the firm pen nib moving back and forth writing saying whatever comes / stop:
a WALL around
text ———————————————————— signature
anonymous scribes: ersonal prono.

Skin where hard-line records mnemonic signs of piercing clinches are inscribed as they happen, in my shoulder; as metaphoric as all this world of evidences strung together subway style, underground anyway.

Tactile hum of sounds whirling round my ear. Abrasive.

Reverberant in the vast virgin thereabouts pre–November 27, 1943 (the text imagines no more than its experience). Aleph – death and survival through which to reach unobstructed clarity in all this. The plunge. Implant myself in the heart of the impenetrable *point.*

Silence on certain restraints, the ones that so violently fan the urge to follow the phantom trace of meaningless babble, freed of all responsibility, executing the overthrow of destructive occult powers with each voluptuous recognition of the self gripped in a state of ecstasy and <u>execution</u>.

Such as drifting into rapture.

The city and yesteryear have faded now from the paper screen. Cherry the redhead wears herself to a frazzle blinking squinting to see if maybe there's rusty red under the white, watching for subtle shades and effects of forms stirring behind the sorry play of empty space to be filled.

DRAWER

## CHAPTER TWO

Any fictional form but factual sequence too. Thus April 22, 1942, five days before the plebiscite, 20,000 *persons* are assembled at the Atwater market. Intrigue is rife. Nothing new but fiction and rattling of bones; chance signs, mysteries, high drama brewed to taste as if to shape a composition from time / on / time holding back the straw that could break the camel's back.

Heads move constantly. The moment is adrift in the folds of cloth coats rubbing together this wartime evening in the unspoken urgency of electing each his special permanent place in the land. Jigging heads (their number creates a state of unsuspected euphoria the very moment of treachery) wartime shell-shaped heads, swelling ears ... jarred by rumbling screeching endless empty Montréal Tramways cars – bane of the French-speaking orators.[1]

Skirmish and ... arms reach out and fall violently on heads ... the sidewalk and horse crap. Ellipse, hustle roughly prodded 'think I passed out getting in the police wagon. I think.' And that's the end of it ... diversion, curiosity, military convoy to be watched parading intestine style or nooselike in the market square.......................................................

... right beside the police station and the bowling alley. *Men* are recruited there during the little town's descriptive game: situated less than twenty miles from Montréal, the town of Beauharnois boasts two major industries ...

[1] On the evening of the protest meeting that took place on February 11, 1942, at the Jean Talon Market, attended by 10,000 people, a constant stream of empty Montréal Tramways steetcars passed not far from the meeting to prevent the speakers from being heard by the crowd.

ENTRANCE, a bowling alley and its fury of senseless noise around balls rolling endlessly toward teetering pins. 'There's the soldiers, two cream sodas, Evalinda. Betcha a game it's yer Momo's turn next week.' 'Don't gimme that' pronounced across the countertop. Conversation all around the alleys ... the words crumble: the bowling alley is a huge deserted beach where scenes of reality brew and composites of potential images take form, in infinite variations around the alley and the GRILL an infamous place in Albina's <u>pious</u> old mind out there on the second range just beyond the village; between the alley and the grill the paths are beaten wide 'cause you gotta look like what you are: cattle and beef <u>meat and grill cannon fodder blast between the eyes meat and too much such cannon grill</u>.

EXIT, 'that way if ya finished yer game.' The main street by the park; from there you can see the river and the islands, tranquil nature undisturbed by fishing boats or tankers, islands not far off. Khaki tents in the market square, officers with officious airs barking the word ORDER all over the place 'like goddamn loonies.'

Standing and watching the word river, and the islands not far off.

Maurice's truck comes by at last, on the way to Ville Lasalle with tomato plants.

The redhead sitting on the sofa, arms and hands and fingers cramped, studies an ashtray in front of her, crystal iridescent flower, contemplates the equivalences of colours. Between the eye and the object, a distance travelled at one's risk and peril of surreptitious rumblings foreign to the ear, of the left hand for example moving suddenly. She says, 'I'm not shaking, it's my whole body vibrating.' Excitement fills her with chills with fire, floats her far from reality like seaweed tossed by a frenzied sea like hair of dantesque red (mane-horse-gallop-fury-wild-freedom) necessary process for sustaining unripe images like Gleason's, king of spades with predatory eye, magnificently sodomising the redhead laid on tulip stems on flowered sheet.

Network of thighs about as delicate as muscular projected in the copulatory act, like a twosome of trapeze artists, she writes about the word network so as to give the story continuity. 'Pure madness' – we learn to read together after all – an attempt at corruption, word for word, executed as the occasion arises, hands and fingers skilled in the pleasure of effect confronting the networks (from red to mauve) esoteric ramifications of the lines of the hand, folds that move on the stomach in the languid aftermath, undulatory traces of that same white substance slipping gently toward the permanent reality of death.

Now in 'forty-two all <u>that</u> stood the test of time and orgasm. Such giddy sensations, with in mind the focus contours of a life to live out to its end, kept returning astonishing the character played by a woman of thirty.

Now as then behind the PRODUCTION factories, the men roll themselves a 'good' cigarette, thinking: bam crack oof uh grrr, thoughtfully. Above their heads the letters crowd together caught in a threatening loop. COMIC STRIP.

A celebration of imagery or … apathy for output and production stirs in their eyes; imagery coloured by thoughts churning in bodies male and female at coffee breaks and the ends of working days, to the shrill tune of the factory whistle spewed above the factory a trace almost locomotive smoke in the wind, longing to get out of there and not come back.

Insistence on electrocuting perforating thoughts of the insane abyss of pleasure. That's what arouses attention: material good for orgiastic consumption (EXCESSIVE USE OF WHAT ONE LIKES) gnawing presence pervading in the neck.

The redhead takes in the presence of sketches and outlines littering the work table. The illusion is perfect; the paper dims, numerical production from zero to vertical one bent in, say, eight other ways so as to proceed with the precise calculation of data which would justify the improvisation.

Self-generated mathematical delirium focus of imagination, of productive effusions also awe-inspiring prospects because *I* bring them to bear on the ineffable world of conquest.

Fear of looking closely at the one who (as can be seen by looking in the mirror) is engaged in writing. Stare at her face until she notices something and enters bodily into an embarrassing complicity in which seconds are prolonged without one's knowing whether this EVENT satisfies the desire or renews it cumbersome like an unusable weapon.

At this point I should perhaps tell a story of I you he we and other plurals recounting one by one all the phases of the enchantment, reconstructing the play of words and of gestures and their consequences in the quebec microcosm; all the phases in the destruction of the he's and she's, braving each reprieve until the narration finally and surely comes to an end. Time and collective animation, and their recording, pursue their course.

GRAFFITI (plural) GRAFFITO (sing).

One or other on the rotting wood fence, on the piss-green doors of toilet cubicles.

MANGE D'LA MARDE Hostie

invocation of excrement, the eating of and sacraments always enigmatic and also representation

CUL CROSSÉ PAR EN AVANT PAR EN ARRIÈRE

FUCK YOU

to be inscribed out of context on paper when words of that ilk ought to be scratched in hard opaque surfaces so that no one could (or even think they could) extract the letters one by one as if to remove them from decent view, from the obscene hand which might linger caressing the little damp gashes laid bare there for all to see who care

VA CHIER P'TITE PLOTTE A JOHNNY

an invitation to a little slut to go shit. Everyday humdrum overthrowing order and *distinction* established in four walls, and elsewhere than on the wall the handwriting shows in broad slaps of paint across a politician's mouth

Le QUÉBEC AUX QUÉBECOIS

on his eye TRAÎTRE between his teeth, the phallic Independence I lifting (an impression) the black freshly daubed moustache.

The crowd because without it nothing is justifiable. Frenzy, confrontation. RESPONSE. Back to square one and all that must go to stem the spate of disharmonies in the age-old habit of writing <u>like</u> we talk.

The crowd (how many are there?) BEFORE always before the something to confront with oneself among others with others before City Hall before parliament or neon Seven-Ups or the barricades *yet*.

Text because the references are too easy to manipulate. Places of encounter 'bring on the drinks' ..................................................................... Something to get across the textual allusions, primary source quotations from line one and face to face defying the phony wooden muscles outstretched brandished here there and everywhere.

Questions of references: for the moment these those in the mêlée on both sides in the sense that words get to be no more than slogans snarled between teeth, crusted on lips.

The other crowd too that can't get the spirit of the thing without hidden motives of self DISPLAY.

Contrast in a text already running dry through overuse of words responding not with pleasure at all but pigheadedness in willing pleasure 'pretending that the gang's all here so an orgy's in order.' If only once there's no pretense of cause, then *crowd* may be written with reference only to pleasure in the text.

What strikes and unfurls overflows the frightful limit more than the mirror and the second look it makes you take, sight struggle inside the wall reflecting gradually caught in the oval from / what secret? / you see plenty of other things too but that crowds are not all the same no way the same when they're making HISTORY (hieroglyphics on what surface when you think of it? – to be decided as events unfold [there must be surfaces as much as compasses for scratching them]).

Crowd / surface there crowds submerge, or a symbolic number descends toward – –

Even if only an illusion, being inscribed here in such an imperfect place as euphoria in textual form if one is willing to add a bit of what is said transcribed transformed thus the word crowd couched hovering in the horizontal version of the atmosphere that emanates on nights of mass meetings / you meet all kinds at times like that.

The pattern the die elbow to elbow. Sure enough 'something' is worn away from the originality roars horribly in the atmosphere, faces transform magma 'I think nothing but fire these days' EXIT.

RED-EXIT cardinal points sentinels.

The impression rather than the true image of … then suddenly (the place the Forum, pop show) hands above supplicating heads toward *le* stage HOSTIE!

LE STAGE HOSTIE expression imposed by the cultural context as initial reflex. Stage floor, smooth surface, guidemarks to move along / oh how we'd like to see the star mated with another star during the SHOW ... the sounds come in separate rooms around the ears of each receiving singular lapping up the crowd sound. We imagine we're at the Forum in the valley, the pit, the rink. And places of fire begin all over piercing to confuse the blackness. Multiple fires held at arm's length.

Absolutely describable; the thirsty paper drinks black soaks up fluid and germinates letters (splash) word for word I we back to the start of the text recounting with absolute authority the years lived from 1941 to '71.

Delve into, drain the pleasure at its most intense the deafening image and the very essence of a show's appeal.

Reference: understand that *wave* at the source of what is signified 'I'm quite old enough to touch another woman' reference to the mirror, episode of 'never felt anything so soft.'

Crowd multiplication of senses approaching sign IN.<br>a leg caressed while he lights<br>a cigarette.

Amplified sound of senses adapting to the cold fire of noise collective apprenticeship in the search for crowd pleasure effects.

A question arising when touching on multiplicity. The number among the staggering number of beings outlined on the retina, sometimes separate, almost always lost in the reality of Montréalers pouring their doubles one by one on *the mimicking surface of the mirror paper*, taking all of them in at a glance and in prose made of resistance and abandon.

Because wanting one thing means unconditionally sensing the reality of its opposite, and by that very fact formulating an impossible concordance of language to fit what has to emerge as some instance of pleasure.

Overlapping factors: restlessness in the line of crowding mass sombre point because of number.

Sombre point identified: enveloping stirring blotch darkness lingering there at length barely moving impregnating space with flux.

From sombre to rusty red turning back to an exploration of particular acts: play of anecdotes the better to pinpoint the environment words and entire passages spawned; they'd be written reproducing in their rhythm the slow calligraphic movements that go with their inscription.

Bluff, starting with that like the eerie whistle of a .22 slug amid the buzz at the cheerful friendly 'barbotte' on Papineau Street. Bluff oozing like pus from the whole room, wounds in necks; vampires on the prowl watching the colour of the folding money and the shiny coins strewn on the table, on the green felt (a green that bathes the eye succulent seductive shadow, *meadow* green crowning the array of colours or flowers of the fields; green of a sudden soothing or ominous ['what if I go home stark naked']) around it players smile and brood in the anonymity and majestic arrogance of clandestinity.

A glance then play. Cards knaves queens red or losers reappraised in a language of the people but foreign to the custom whereby in order to communicate one has to talk like everybody else. Surface atmosphere dream like Rodolphe's imagining his victory over Edmond after five years of weekly defeat.

Small room; today it's the kitchen. Yesterday the 'dicks' padlocked the bedroom door. 'They tip us off anytime they're gonna raid.'

Léo loses, loses, wins then asks for more chips and puts them by the sink. White and soft clunk of wooden chip. Hot coffee, gros gin spilled on the felt cloth, between brown suspenders and on Pierre's white shirt.

A private place familiar to initiates, on the inside shiny like a new vinyl floor. Trademarks on the walls; Black Horse and calendar, crucifix; smell of cigars, half-eaten apple on the corner of table no. 6, description without solution of the dream world fashioned from the other world, the real one, where one wouldn't dream of invading a woman's bingo game with its stale nostalgic air 'might as well pass the time while we wait.'

Poker face and agile fingers. Always the fear of the classic cardshark (silent stranger, tattooed, shifty-eyed) pure invention made of adjectives and coincidence. A preserved specimen image poking through the screen on which the line of chance is already traced with its Straights and Royal Flushes winning species in hard cash.

Outside the 'barbotte' two Quacks pass hips swinging under their unbecoming uniforms, already weighing their words before reporting to the lecherous Captain Larouche of the Van Doos.

Today as it happens, having contemplated the crowd the redhead is considering returning to the private place that gratifies her so. An ambiance propitious to desire and its corridors of fantasy. Imagining with eye and hand and a dreadful urge to brave all, to lose herself there (inside her the provocative *germ* of near-frenzy, of dangerous liaisons). To be perilously at the brink of. Ravaging the page with herself, reflecting that temptation is an open door to all sensations of fulfillment.

Manifestation of south-shore suburban transgression in Brossard – version told at the provincial Police Station; Cherry surmises that this time silence won't get her out of the fix she's in. Words: say all, tell all, reveal all till they're saturated hearing stories of blow jobs, sodomy, kinky whippings over tender young backs … in lady-like terms … like poor tired little penis.

Transgression in words how and once it's written what is it if not violence by the writer exploring, if not violence by whatever stands in the way of conquest, of domination over the self, and over others I'll be told.

It might be written too that to tell the truth Cherry wasn't really involved just visiting in that little suburban town lit like a tombstone.

Rain, a mirror in each puddle.

Dreams and drawers closed again. Watchful-waitress EYE.

Scars / tattoos, something not unlike writing being traces and effect of language in the skin through play of dotted lines or incision by metal in the flesh (Hawaiian dancer, arrow-pierced heart or cobra) bare chest, belted corpulent waist, Saint-Laurent Main, picture-plastered shop; 'Special price to musclemen.' POSTER. 'If it hurts smoke a joint.' 'You got a fine body bejesus.'

CLOSED: the tattooer's tattooing the too fat cat the big shot of the Main.

Scene unchanged the quadrilateral (streets) *yellow circle* on the map *misshapen eye* – criss-cross of fuzzy lines: Montréal – thousands joined by telephone lines (the network); absolute space reduced to a telephone book a little organism feeding the city with its coded symbols.

Word association, password combination set hard in the memory, beautiful symbols. Parallels/perpendiculars coming into focus with concentrated looking at the yellow, the circle, the precise location looked for.

Exemplary rusty red target of a watery barrage from the sky ('mobile walls of rain' I'll soon be thinking). Hair (each strand, its role in the structure of the whole only too alive moving in caressing hands as to chords of Latin-American music syncopated breathless uh-uh; plexus [interlacing vessels, journey]) hallucin ........................ .............................. channel of lifeblood and a vague wave, the journey of novelistic fiction in the human body, Saturn rings turning BLACKOUT the network once again blood vessels clear red or rusty, spacelike.

Alcohol (Sainte-Catherine Street) noises, a smell of Acapulco Gold.

Every alcohol-infiltrated vein burning impurities, burning the inner body, consuming it like incense watched by the strange eye of the kingfisher or could it be a decorative Season's Greetings on the wall that catches and provokes the eye, brilliant red and evergreen boughs. White; the alcohol pervades, reaches the broad spaces inside, nautical and fabulous.

Nineteen hundred and forty-one and remembrance of a text destined to mark a two-fold temporal reality before and now in the familiar but also unsuspected Montréal of conscription days.

For an ABC of a certain collective life in the city as lived at the time but to emerge later and elsewhere in a sense full of purpose. Here however there'll be no talk except to consider two *proper* nouns (Cherry and Gleason) and a few **common** nouns names of streets and public places.

The etc. of thought in a difficult text, *terrifying* urges to harp on the *long legs of desire* pure fiction of ordinary words absorbing more than the hypnotic pendulum.

Space; decorative alphabet crowning west-end department stores.

Sliding doors, open windows at spring-cleaning time, space, the city, the *tentacular* metropolis as in a book on American architecture which if paid more attention to would sow panic *inside* a body spent / spending its reserves of energy bit by bit.

..................................................................................

Lugubrious rings lycanthropic eyes above the city. Aggression as in a bad dream in which Cherry could lose life the ultimate right majestically with her whole body to love the mask and velvet pelt of the wolf-man devouring (figures of speech) with his eyes the hot-dog eaters issuing contentedly from the A&W.

Probe with infinite care the meaning of the various airs she puts on daily playing the continuing role of correspondent.

Mail-text-form to fill out. Spinning letters inscribed; invade the fictional almanac and attack the nitty-gritty the subject, positive pickup (comparison with) the needle on the black plastic surface of the disk. Stylus.

Proliferation of India inks in signals – multiplicity of scattered lines rearranged – suddenly, which form a mass of senses, an agglomeration of infinite beauties (bird's eye view of) canvas and patch of stimulus gradually transforming the viewer's eager eye into an artist's.

Punctuation nil, initial reflex … followed by an express and formulated urge to prepare the ground for exploratory plays.

Plan for one like any profound intense sleep; dark trace of words inward curve to the rosy channel of cerebral circumvolutions.

Flooded with non-visual images, images running phenomenally wanton on the scalp, differentiated from retinal intuitions, from the moisture that turns them to a carnival of uncertain hues.

… from delights new-discovered linking I and we to the vulnerability of one's temples.

Use of symbols, the ones above the letters (on a typewriter keyboard) slipped into the spaces between the words.

Composition become space and silence between the sounds of words, knocking reality from its pedestal (image of smooth plexiglass and fibre binding or is it the eye caressing the FIBRE (material) that binds d (fib) Konstruktion.

Space-word: interval prolonged till all resistance fades so the thought advances, 'so' that makes the tacit link, if one likes, to something luminously obvious in the precise order of juxtaposition of obvious pleasures to which no character in 1941 or today or any fictitious person could HOLD A CANDLE 'when I give it the works.'

# CHAPTER FOUR

Incitement to follow the flow, the bustle of people going somewhere or just walking in Phillips Square. A simple circulatory movement, and the starchy circumference of department stores catches the easily influenced eye on this the evening of the Proclamation of the War Measures Act. 'Some people say … ' – 'What d'you expect, we're at war.'

On their delivery route, a milkman's horse is racing an iceman's. The streets are wide, giving rein to imagination and chalk graffiti. 'Pierre loves Pierre' like a monstrous piece of gossip. Private Lebrun gives voice to a plaintive ballad in the corner restaurant while Ginette, who installs fabric on the frames of aeroplanes, counts her savings and thinks over the proposal she's had from the little blond Saint-Denis Street boy. Goose pimples, restless epidermis, 'so what? Oughta get married though … hope there's some wedding rings left at the jeweller's.'

In front of the Chénier monument a bum bundled up like a polar bear, scarf flapping, sounds off interminably at the red maple autumnal beside him, its leaves not falling fast enough to suit him and his mind-boggling drinker's tempo. Since the world began the old souse Charland has come to sit every evening by the monument, gazing at it with haggard face as though it were Chénier himself or perhaps the English still come bursting all too violently into his memory.

From behind his hornrimmed glasses Charland studies the situation; the monument, the bridge not far off, the neighbourhood children. He rails for nothing, with a stray dog there in front of him eating a dry hotdog off the endless curb.

Buildings, streets, things, all seem perpendicular to one another. A vast array of little crosses seen from a window from which someone is leaning now, against the ledge of weathered cement soiled white by carrier pigeons which sooner or later will take off for Halifax and elsewhere on their way to the far-flung beaches of Normandy with their deserted casinos.

Text and memory, book-ends on the mantle-piece in a Craig Street shop window. *Junk* invades the eye, junk, perchance to buy if the owner doesn't overdo either his praise of the junk or his price.

Bustle, clattering tramcars; a jelly bean deep in his pocket, Charland teeters.

Word for word within the plot, the narration of whose principal events take place in Montréal at two precise points in time with lapses of silence inside the compact mass of **black** thoughts (IN PRINT).

Plea by the eye [i] from a sense for sense to what is going on in certain surroundings centre of attraction of lucid skin [if that is, then what is to come has already been written / read].

All things that return to mind are muted in the daily figuration of calligraphic back-and-forth in which a line seething with bits of sentences BEHIND THE NOTRE DAME STREET FACTORIES confuses the eye so thoroughly one really can't be sure what form what character one has settled on to impart it all.

From incitement [eye-opening] to informing by the expedient of writing in perfectly natural <u>train</u> of thought informing DIFFERENTLY dropping *loose* gratuitous signs of sense and possibility.

'O.K. so we're tough you 'n' me, but that there stiff last night, who wuz it?' as in narration built of juxtapositions, with emphasis mostly on the juxtaposition and always following the *trace* and catching the eye by jiggling a few <u>vandalous phrases</u> of oblique significance as in something crossed out.

Stupefaction: watching numbed by a kind of nerve centre inhibition, the images heeded so little, measured so little to one's heartbeat, that around the self, in the language chosen, colours and words come crowding which don't go together but once they're put together complete each other perfectly, sodomites, inFORMing bodies, imprinting them horizontally in the mold ... the bodies fall thick and beautiful to the tune of the typewriter tapping (accènts acute and circumflêx).

Fade in on hair (the word) on the surface / if the sense could designate a geography in the mute lines of the orb of the eye, blues, reds, veinlike traces, then (marks the continuity) … / shining oily / but if rusty red becomes something other than hair HOW is the metamorphosis to be interrupted and the wave furrowing <u>one's</u> forehead checked, there above the eyebrow drawn like an anomaly inside a wrinkle.

(Pron. / auxilliary) walks the city trying to keep silent between Delormier and the Main (from north to south, parallels don't mean nearly as much). People-cages and metaphors abound (tourists gape, swallowing flies and antiquated old-world French terms 'le kartier fransay oh yeah!'

Long march on Montréal by a determined walker beaten (through huffs and puffs his stumbling bilingualism explained: the gorgon, multiple tongues in her hair moving / touching if you consider the light in those eyes beneath the waving hair) THUNDERING ONOMATOPOEIAS (Plessis Street) seven *Cobras* roar by, asses tight on the seats of their bikes.

Elements of the EVENT: establish a relationship between Cherry, the amount of dye in her hair, Gleason's virility, also of course (nineteen hundred and forty-one) as isolated (point of) reference (point) on the phallic I in graffiti … childish scrawls inventing a new game of exploration with clues to follow (?!:$). Trails and clues indelible in the memory lead to the scrapheap behind the 'blasted' factory belching black smoke. Remembering this recitation:

**'Consentez-vous à libérer le gouvernement de toute obligation résultant d'engagements antérieurs restraignant les méthodes de mobilisation pour le service militaire? (27 avril, 1942)'.**

Surface and transparency: objects under glass (doll, perfume [bottle of], pen, key-ring, necklace) to be lifted with aluminum tongs hanging from a chain. *A dime, a flop, another dime, another flop.*

Sunday, yesterday afternoon, it must have been about five o'clock; a fanciful jumble of intentions and come and go (after the dime machine bit) all about a word (penis) in the mouth.

Illustration streaked all over the surface of play and over most of the images in this calligraphic assemblage. Pauses: man in the crowd, kneeling woman (fellatio) and other many other amorous poses / PAUSES extirpated from daily life in order to know their pangs (quickened heartbeat, rush of blood through delicate tissues and membranes) the delicious consequence.

An inner current, a circulating image, oblique words that tell of it and intrude on the body of the image soon confounding it with the atmosphere it exudes. Shadows swell, their breathing unseen by the eye but perceived, a bewildering encounter between two subepidermal mysteries (far beyond the reality of language).

..............................................................................

epidermis and camouflage ('you wouldn't know her') a perfect ruse for Gleason who dares not touch and recognize.

And then he finds himself on the brink of tears.

It's here the knavery begins, words slipped in by stealth by the anonymous but potent presence that always imposes its own translation *poetic remembrance* in italics; there is a potency in the art of camouflage. The sovereign eye knows where to find the crack the weak point and make it the hub of ludic anarchy – such literary artistry.

# CHAPTER FIVE

The façade of Windsor Station is quite old. The porters in blue are black; the people giving tips are white, conscripts and volunteers, and leaving for Halifax. Trains arrive and depart. Ginette has come to meet Pierre of Saint-Denis Street. Tales of daring, fictional and in the cards. Jules Verne / Walter Mitty on the station platform. 'I saw him I tell you. Look, it IS Edmond.' Fantasy and portions of truth. Loudspeakers broadcast English sounds that metamorphose, by chance as Pierre of Saint-Denis Street sets his foot on the second step of the railway car, into Lili, preying mantis, Dietrich, Marlene nectar gathering among the many sexes male and virgin. Warm soft female balm 'What more can a guy want!'

Here we see mere episodes of impersonal allegiance to the Prime Minister's decree advancing toward the railway cars, looking for a window seat the better to wave (biting their lips) to those staying behind to work and make babies.

**The ring of iron-clad heels** on terrazzo the chequerboard station concourse, elbow-jabs handshakes and kisses. **The ring of iron-clad heels on the chequerboard** advance and capture, losers win; officers stop and pose in front of their railway car for a picture. Front page of the Gazette, first edition: SEVEN OFFICERS KILLED BY LUNATIC; picture, corpses, chortling brooks of blood. Inset left corner, face of the suspect, the maniac assumed to be the perpetrator of the crime, an east-end wino, 'one of those French Canadians who live like animals near the bridge.'

Above the crowd of soldiers' relatives and friends the station clock shows its hands; killing time, Edmond studies it as if it were a race sheet showing, in order of calculated chances of victory, the names of horses running at the Aqualiente track in Mexico over the next three weeks.[1]

[1] During the war, all American racetracks were closed and Montréal's (clandestine) gamblers resigned themselves perforce to betting on horses running in Mexico. Race results took four hours to arrive.

So rusty red inscribes hair and dye and grotesque too in the text and the past. Handled (like plasticene) and written (laid on a surface) rusty red that ought to arouse manifold interpretations and offers perhaps just one; but when repeated, should it be singular or plural.............................................................................
when you *think* about it (hanging on the thread of the story, like a sleepy spider) ...

A circumscribed zone containing linguistic deviations and intentions to put words on paper; circumscribed, to be described, placed before the reading eye; its dimensions and possibilities for interplay of (inexhaustible) meanings. ZONE; place of betwixt and between, between the brief yes and no shorn of all tone, hence zone place of atmosphere open to any interpretation or intervention.

Traced (signed) on the surface, a graphic approximation of thoughts receding and returning. Being such (thoughts): short circuit / flash; (insane) almost hazardous demonstration.

Very breathless and very redhead in the taxi taking her from downtown (west) to Saint-André Street (room to rent) in the back seat, very irked by the driver's leer in the rearview mirror 'Cigarette?' The leather sticks to her thighs and holds them down, activates, slowly dampens her pants. Very enravished, lounging on the moleskin (having come) relaxed spinning out the sweetness of it with reiteration of the definition: 'long combing wave produced in certain estuaries by the meeting of ebb and flow.' Tidal bore.

To sow *trouble* taken literally: plan embodying personal risk (smile and snarl each in turn exorcising the other / important signs ramified proceeding toward the buccal exit / spoken signals) confounded by all that daily practice in hatching (TROUBLE MAKER) effects with words.

*Forthcoming* in the trouble-sowing play, transparent three-dimensional alphabets; equivocal at the very least.

Bloody Mary the red sticks on the retina. MANIFESTO. It adds I have the impression that 'my inspiration is afloat somewhere in the room.' Music brought that on yet I quote from source, departing somewhat from the text to be sure.

Paragraph.

Vulva and glans emerging in the light. On the retina.

Cartridge: 'place the cartridge either end first in the body of the pen.' Accessory essential to the continuation of the event the flow of intertwining lines, POX on the click or rather the requisite resolve as though luxuriating and infuriating went together, ensued without conjunction in one's mind and ran together outside the text    marginal gripping too much in the thoracic cage, that void of inspiration spent.

Spotlight on the initial rusty red. Next page.

Resistance of the ground against her flat mat back on the sands of Oka by the lake by its glare of blue against its cloudless double.

A bottle of Black Horse on the shore, incongruous with the sand and lapping water … at the hour when sailboats drop their sails and glide toward the forest edge and evergreen boughs (in Cherry's armpits humidity and scent of wood) ................................ ............................ on the road a few miles later, through squinting half-closed eyes open country and a few wide-brimmed hats sighted near Saint-Eustache. Safety catch. Someone must have fired; 'Came from there for sure. Of course, it's the season.' AUTUMN.

Put boat and oar in the calligraphic bl to let what's waiting there beneath the skin fill and be filled before luminating the words and surfaces we happen to offer smooth burnished smoother still (hot wet palm) the snare of dual appearance / appurtenance of textures (canvas for example).

Calling up the past indeed by examining the ecchymosis, bl skin turned blue more precisely like the violets in Purple Garden (neon).

Diagonal / a slice of yesterday's everyday life (classified relics) DOWNTOWN parallel strings of onions, US.

A twist of tell me a story of rusty red in a maze of clever expressions 'I get an eyeful' whenever I read or after anyway.

Blank space.

Sunday singular somnolent day. Picture image and violence curve of neck picture of singular desire (rape), of coarse hand on that graceful if slightly grubby neck.

Laid out full length of the word body on a surface tender spring grass Cherry poses and click COVER girl on all the newsstands to be viewed with jaundiced eye rusty red by passersby and foxy exiles in Greater Montréal.

Rusty red imbibed as in blotting paper and rough texture in the porous textual material, by that insinuating that any bookish demonstration infiltrates the immediate entourage of more or less anonymous exposures ‘portrait of a redhead at suppertime’ imagination drifting off occasionally in midstream to light on something else, long enough for an excuse to be alone.

Here rests the scrutinizing eye.

Persistent pangs the breast their source and target (an avalanche but off a duck's back), well and truly parenthetic in the weft (the goal and pleasure) of interwoven words.

Pangs to see it all pour out pouring sp-sperm begging to be spoken.

Redhead Cherry in name alone, the lexicon of rusty red simply must be made (small personal adventure; sequential peradventure).

Let EAST (direction) be taken as a manifestation of a CULTURAL offense (sequelae, sequelae … ). WE anonymous pops up anyway as part of a play of characters. TYPESETTER: 'It's Friday and we got Monday off.'

Competition from space little black book and telephone. For her finger enters each little plastic circle and touches the three letters and the digit printed in black, works best that way. She dials (composes) it's visible the number in her head. The code and its evolution; the network … at the other end of the WIRE yakkity-yak comunication.

Acts and cultural acts and animal cheery old imaginary legendary bestiary and subliminal cyclic carousel of colours: at the Faisan Doré something's left from '43 seen with half-closed eye then wide open minutes later he perceives himself in the barroom mirror white like a gravesheet perceives it was first rusty red he'd seen then heard the conscript's voice.

# French Kiss, or, A Pang's Progress

by Nicole Brossard
translated by Patricia Claxton

*French Kiss, or, A Pang's Progress* is a translation of *French Kiss: étreinte–exploration*, which was first published in 1974 by Editions du Jour.



This translation was first published as *French Kiss* in 1986 by Coach House Press as part of the Quebec Translations series, edited by Barbara Godard and Frank Davey. A third edition with some corrections was printed in 1988.

## Translator's Foreword

With the author's full agreement, this translation is a little more accessible than the underlying French, which is to say, less hermetic. But only to a point, for there is much to be found beneath the apparent surface of Nicole Brossard's book, and so it must remain.

In case the reader may wonder how authentic the translation of historical quotations may be, the fragment on the final page is 99% pure, being almost totally faithful to Richard Hakluyt's translation, published first in 1600, of the *Relation of Iames Cartiers discouery and Nauigation to the Newfoundlands, by him named New France*. In typically sixteenth-century fashion, Hakluyt was quite inconsistent in his spelling, and most unobligingly modern with some of the words in this fragment; the 1% impurity is in the more picturesque spelling of those words, transferred from elsewhere in Hakluyt's own text. The translation of other historical fragments is mine, with spelling consistent with that found in English texts of the parallel historical period.

There are occasional unobtrusive aids for readers who know Montréal only slightly or not at all, and similarly with allusions to French and Québécois literature and history. The characters' names have not been anglicized because their owners belong intrinsically to Montréal's long-disadvantaged French-speaking majority. As for the apparently English name Lucy Savage, whatever inspiration and symbolism the reader finds in it will probably be right. However, the physical and psychological opposition of east and west in the city (east of Bleury Street and west of it) should not be overlooked; when not in the foreground it is an essential part of a backdrop which remains despite changes of scene.

Small capitals indicate words and phrases that Brossard has consciously used in English in her French text, demonstrating how English so pervades French speakers of Montréal that a writer may feel it natural to change horses briefly in midstream from time to time. These phenomena are different though not always totally distinct from the anglicisms which typically pepper Québécois speech. Which uglify it according to some. Which give it much of its earthy vigour according to others.

Occasional typograpical errors have needed correcting in the translation process. Some of these have prompted recourse to the manuscript, which resides in Québec's Bibliothèque nationale along with the pages and pages of orderly notes from which the French text was constructed. One such correction arises from a contradiction between the book's first and second editions; both the manuscript and typescript vindicate the first, by Les Editions du Jour, which gives *liido*, as opposed to *libido* in the Quinze edition.

While this English text may be a little more accessible than the underlying French, if it has succeeded in its purpose the character of the book in other respects remains intact.

Nicole Brossard writes without compulsion to conform to the dictates of linearity or conventional rules of language. Moreover she does not demand that her readers think or feel precisely this or that; she sketches bare outlines, fleeting impressions of what her senses and sensitivity perceive as she develops her word plays and word associations. Word plays and word associations are the meat of this book. It is built on them. It follows where they lead. In English they rarely originate or develop in the same way or lead in the same direction as they do in French. Yet, since in English they must prompt the same responses in the reader as they do in French, they must touch base constantly with the French text. As one might suspect, they are often quite different. The modern Bible scholar and translator Eugene Nida has compared solving a stubborn translation problem with crossing a turbulent river, when, in order to reach one's destination directly opposite on the other side, one needs to search some distance up- or down-stream to find a fording place.

Given inescapable differences in cultural and linguistic outlook and hence resources, from the translator's point of view such translation will yield weaker impact at certain points than one might wish, try as one will. But turn the corner to another sentence or paragraph, and there, sometimes plain to see but more often partly hidden, one may find a perfect plum of an opportunity, sometimes even more apt for the situation than what has been available in the source language for the underlying text. These do not turn up at every page, but blessedly they do occur. Translation theorists call this kind of thing 'compensation,' the recompense, or perhaps atonement, for those unavoidable degrees of semantic loss incurred elsewhere in a text.

I have used the terms 'word plays' and 'word associations' arbitrarily and specifically in the present context, meaning them to be understood as discrete but related. Word plays are in the language itself; they may consist of common, everyday metaphors, even clichés, or they may be unfamiliar, perhaps arcane, but the language, be it French or English, has registered them; they are everyone's word associations, so to speak. What I have called word associations here are Brossard's own word associations, intensely personal ones and rich with her own prolific imagination; they are not associations that would occur in the normal course to me, the translator, or to you, the reader, if left to our own devices. The word plays are tools that anyone might pick up and use; the word associations are uniquely hers.

How faithful this book is to the other depends on what one looks for in faithfulness. Many obvious transitions have been set aside because they mislead, or because there is a nuance to be respected. For me, the key is whether this text prompts the same responses in the reader, word play by word play, image by image, setting by setting, as the French text does in a native French speaker. An image that stirs a French reader yet leaves an English reader intellectually informed but unmoved is not an adequately translated image. One thing is certain; the more creatively imaginative the underlying work, the more subjective will be the act of translating it. Since *French Kiss* in French is highly imaginative, and particularly since word plays and word associations are central to it, this translation is very subjective indeed. It has therefore been severely scrutinized jointly by author and translator to make sure that the subjective content remains in keeping with the underlying work. I am grateful to Nicole Brossard for the vast amount of time and patience she has devoted to a side-by-side reading of the two texts in order to ensure that they really do match, that her intentions are achieved, that each word play and association, each image, abstraction and conveyance of mood or atmosphere is consistent with her own thinking.

Patricia Claxton
November 1985

## Once

Ride astride grammar. I spread myself, eager, inconsequential and desire.

Destination the point of furthest (though reversible) displacement of my conscious state. Slow progressive irrigations in the city and in my breast.

Words get confused
So hotly used

Madness, vague rapturous condition, is that really all there is in the soft yellow surface of a morning egg? Madness or whatever it is in one's breast but isn't transparent in Camomille, that gradually leads her on and lets her have a hand in the jolt I'm going to get backfire style. In the story's telling, fictional … and contrivances … glowing volatile in darkness that could be perhaps the dark of night amid a thousand conifers.

The words *body* and *city* get confused and mingled with a geography; maps or is it cards on the table, anatomical diagrams, systems.

And Camomille intervenes, forcing the I, making circumstances that require her presence in this text. Not a parasitic chess-game I but an I that's exploring, autonomous, anarchistic

and spans all the dimensions of Camomille's worlds, and my own, ambiguous one.

We enter with the reading of an image: twelve noon in the body, the liquid play of blood in clockwise circulation, the play of productive and destructive life. Twelve noon beneath the clock, interior mutations, dislikes and likes cartographically deployed. Veins and arteries, lanes and streets. Obsession with the habitation of the self, a body occupied.

An obsession; to be turned paper thin and page like a pregnant silence watched, say, in a poignant scene of agitation, an image of a head moving rhythmic on a moving pillow, a breathing mouth panting emptied of its breath, thirsting (we'll return to those fantasies that infiltrate our breasts with acts and send them prowling round our eyes) thirsting with desire crushed horribly in a vision of a huge round frenetic sun advancing merciless on pupils diameter awash hot lava flowing molding in a mold; ambiant sexuality.

One afternoon when you're trying in mid-centense to figure out why.

Camomille Delphie, fiction's she-wolf, basks contented cool in her self-created shade. Fictional romanticism. There's the merest step it's clear from Camomille to Marielle Desaulniers driving in real life down real Sherbrooke Street's tarmac at forty miles an hour in a Plymouth, an old convertible, purple vintage 1965. The customary route's between a third-floor walkup on Colonial Street and the highrises of Stanley Street. Today it's different, a cruise across the city. The whole length of Sherbrooke Street from one end to the other, east to west. West to east. A carousel of history and geography. Hot currents *savage* ones. FAR EAST, GOING DOWNTOWN FAR AWAY WEST. Motels with crazed and peeling paint. Cheap and flashy neon signs. Marielle drives with leaden eyes.

Verbal bottlenecks. Words and woes get confused. We each have our own equipment for communication. Pages are darkened, scratch scratch blackened toast … Lucy Savage, thirty years old, great-granddaughter of Lucy Stone, late nineteenth-century anti-slaver and feminist. Psychedelic seductive Lucy, imbibed in this text, memory's blotting paper, all-seeing at the nub of it in her role of central character. She sees with tender darting eyes. Savage: undulant amoeba. Life drifts this way and that on an autumn leaf down to dewy lawns or forest floor, is lost and regained through Camomille's fictional lips, now recounting with leer from ear to ear how she's just noticed that Marielle has a younger brother – wicked sexual strategist. Alexandre calls Marielle Elle meaning She for short, and She him Lexa.

## Twice

Keeps pushing pulling inside and out, urgent like arrows and tomahawks, murderous rocks hurled from high on the Plains of Abraham – dangles, Algonquin dance from timbers two feet thick, once whole oaks glowing splendid in the forest the better to satisfy the lusts and fantasies of maidens all too fruitful undisciplined servants to milady's locks and low-cut body-molding gown – billboard. A forest smelling pungently of brick, cool green forest painted on a wall of brick. Along Sherbrooke Street, one by one the forests self-destruct before the eyes of motorists. And setting forth in the wee morning hours of the night, Elle Desaulniers drives melancholia and coffee alternating, each short-circuiting the other, melancholy as in memories and why so many all at once?

Lexa body from antiquity, a Sistine Chapel body – glans held by so many hands (by all those figures), fiction instigators, superman glans. Lexa queen bee in a hive of pleasure. Only the pope's nose knows what the pope knows of such goings on.

An overwhelming hotwave. A heaving swell. Part getaway part chase bowling speed Marielle's in full control of the wheel despite the downpour swilling across the windshield. Down drown beware the multiple raindrop and: – plop p̸ against the glass (shadows of shadows the wipers nose to nose in dance before her eyes). Spatters against the sides. Blow but in quite another sense (brains out that is) – catch fire, press against the side, stick close with coarse hairs and saliva … in the slot … a broad rolling river in flood. Cats and dogs in gobs.

In her head Lexa sticks to the ceiling, a mental image, a fruit, a glans hanging overhead, a luscious plum that should fall of its own accord and not be plucked. Bite. Bight, a bay open to the sea. Green serene Aegean. The clarity of calm. One might have imagined or caught sight of Lexa at Hydra on the rocks, naked, or at La Ronde in the Western Bar Saloon all dandied up, hot pistol on each hip, munching on a piece-a pizza.

Into the labyrinth goes Marielle this brother to discover and parade for Lucy Savage who thenceforth can't detach herself from him till she's sucked him dry like a text to use as massage vibrator and also musical score in a frenzied interplay of sounds and sensibilities – the scenes and symbols binding Camomille and Lucy will need a site of course, a dimension in a society. Since it would be for naught, Camomille and Lucy won't go pointing accusatory fingers at each other for other people's benefit, to scandalize. It's intensity that's scandalous, sweet death all the way, say, from Volos to Skiatos. Who's to say they mightn't be seen abroad, or in Quebec City visiting the Marie de l'Incarnation Museum, reviving with graphic pun the bolstered breast of 'a young widow of quality,' Madame de la Peltrie. A pun one could imagine taking shelter from the rains and snow under the Porte Saint-Jacques.

Alexandre looks up. His friend, *Geor*graphy says he, points to shapes still plain to see of two bald heads in close proximity, shining pates below a sweep of flowing locks. Georges admires his ingenuity, the artist tit-man wag. Lexa's thinking more of getting back to Montréal. In only twenty minutes the next bus leaves.

Montréal Island's eastern tip is where Marielle's excursion, her long drive begins. At a little wooden house she's just dropped off a hitchhiker who's driven with her all the way from Lanoraie. Early fog-bound morning, no rain as yet.

No way she's going home to Colonial Street. Why does Lucy always wear long skirts? Pale Charlemagne Bridge, like an overexposed noonday photograph. Slippery ballroom floor for Meteors, Astres, Demons, Cougars and Cobras surging yellow red on either side of the white line carpeting the scene most incompletely, resembling as they go in leaps and bounds the preposterous shapes of tiger-bugaboos in the field of view … how could ferrets, raccoons, field mice find such easy entry to the landscape in the mind of Elle with foot jammed on the accelerator taking out the memory of a loathsome toad suddenly before her when she was walking teenage dreamy-eyed romantic in the woods the haunt of bums behind her father's house.

'I'm all shook up ...' Never heard it. Well, this one's the most: 'She was just seventeen, y'know what I mean, and the way she looked was way beyond compare ...' That setting's got to go. Heaven's to Betsy one wouldn't dare! To de-scribe is to reanimate an occasion on occasion. Narrator / detonator. They'll hear me coming from afar, conical delirium, they'll see me come in she-wolf's clothes, a narrator set to pounce on any theme or romp. Dear Marielle, you're so good at being two and self-indulgent too that I've quite forgotten Camomille and Lucy my miraculous survivors like organs valuable and genital.

Ride astride syntax. Which bodes an ode or goads me to something anyway at this very early hour my how long it takes to cross the bridge. Now all we need's a unicorn captive in a paddock near the asylum of Saint-Jean-de-Dieu, horn awail, calling to insanity to come and set it free, what could be more natural? Rather than romantic mythic witchery it brings a pang inside, as piercing as uncurbed pain. Now appears the phallus (the Virgin spotted distant in the fog, more phantasmal than the Phantom of the Opera, passive unto eternity).

What time is it, since workingmen are coming out of houses bordering the road. What season, since fires burn all the time from the burn-off stacks of sprawling oil refineries – by night a mighty warship at anchor on dry land the east end of the island.

Marielle's half asleep. Coffee but not now. Coffee, melancholy, I love you Lexa. Why are you sleeping in the corridor? Well, I didn't want to go with Georges, not even with you. Here Lucy Savage butts in: 'What if the corridor were a Venus flytrap?' 'What a bitch you are Lucy dear.'

A red Venus for Lexa. A textual trap to brood about, perchance to knock down or drag out, but whose fecundity will occasion a re-examination of the subject.

'Marielle's no wildflower in my arms.'

Lexa's no insect between my legs.'

Venus and red, a dialectical odyssey in a future future year, a cavity in a vampire's tooth.

'Cut it out, Elle!'

Coffee time.

## Thrice

Transparency and what causes it when my eyes turn to Camomille and find that studying the expression in hers means plunging into a kind of intrigue, some wellspring of anguish it's crystal clear (so many contradictions though). What is it then that seems opaque? Her body of course or else the self-control she exercises when she *hangs in self-absorption* from her lovers, when she breaks and dies with that faculty she has, in every cell, of moving in the *sovereign space* of she, alone, egocentric, perfect in orgasmic joy; or else, while stirring up the fantasies essential to her pleasure, the orgasm she abandons from fatigue, with one syncopated word too much. Her body and its cells evolve, interact, jostle according always to a set of rules. Sometimes to a faster rhythm. Camomille wants Delphie so she'll have perfection in consistency, total sway in her carnal realm. Her possessions are her body, her weapon, and the narcissistic story line of she with exploratory clitoris.

Daily she tests herself. For understanding means using ingenuity, filling one's head with disturbing phantasms, with agitation and serenity as well since Camomille Delphie's fantasies are all bi-polar ones, two-edged swords.

In the single room of her apartment she creates lush green worlds, and others of arid rock. For example, tawny red Rhodisi and resplendent Phlemboukos, celestial rocks, are there to keep her on her rocker.

Camomille all fantasy, fictional or real. She props a hand on a garage wall (anywhere, anywhen, anyhow) vomiting her all, her life, a bellyful; veins of her neck in high relief, total Camomille loses a portion of herself (leaving her whole economy in straits). Heaves and retches. Shudders. She strives for indecency (in terms of self-awareness) with revelation of nutriments mounting to her mouth, parting her lips, pouring sidewalk bound. Subsiding beside her.

Leafy greens. Blobs of food mollusc-like congeal round Delphie's feet. Breathing's easier now.

Amoeboid Lucy, you need to feed on fragmented things. Cut up Lexa or this text in little bits then flow around them gracefully, soothing as water round a pearl, your prey.

This morning Lucy sits across from Camomille, carefully observes her performing the breakfast rite. Down goes the juice, tongue licks from left to right the way one rubs or crosses out, moustache orange like a cat's, eye above, an eye for me to thread you through. Tongue 'a nimble mass of muscle' activates a traffic back and forth, particles of food. Meet up, thrash about, buffet the muscles of the cheeks. Break into speech like English cannonballs nibbling gnawing at the Plains of Abraham. Syllables dilate. Delphie's articulation's bad. Lucy Savage grabs the opportunity, sticks out her tongue, lets Delphie know the tongue she'll use is sharp and curious and out to touch on every surface imaginary or real.

Effort to speak. Camomille salivates. Gets wet. Mucin. The saliva clings to the inner surfaces. Buccal membrane, the phrase alone wafts her to a site of sweet delight where the longest spaces – of undetermined length – at once seem lubrified as for erotic use, an unexplored syntactic slope on which we might however touch and there inconsequentially rub up some urges and convictions. Sparks. Erectile, eremetic narrators we.

Savage with her voyeur's eye fixed on Delphie's mouth, really most provocative as indicator of a panoramic body whence features can be seen. Gay abandon, life, hard knocks all at once. Landscape, a procession of forms like ripplewaves (a word she found while wiggling her toes in the silky sand on Skiatos and thinking curvilinearwave) at the bottom of the sea.

The toast's just right. The succeeding sentence remains to be resolved: delicately arched, Camomille's fingers reduce the toast to crumbs. They work like scissors, cats' tongues, lady fingers, describable by derivative, a visual sensation of little ornamental arcana. On her mouth however a line of bole would be too too arcane, unthinkable at this early hour, though red would in no way be incongruous.

After breakfast we could go to Marielle's. What for? To see Georges and Lexa. Tell me a bit about Georges. Camomille's impression listening to Lucy is that everything's reposing at the bottom of a big glassful of water and dissolving aspirins. Cloudy, in a fog. Marielle's slowed down a bit. Stones, cracks, chaos. Lucy talks, unwinds, lets it out from her reserves of mastery and persuasion. The textual body bubbles (how banal) with copulas and complements rising from the when what how of Marielle and Lexa, of mastering their relationship, and also getting to the bottom of Georges's macho attitude, his 'Gotta fuck you' when he's told, 'Whoa back, don't rush me so.'

The task's to decode this daily life, the values and storylines being played in it. The aspirin's finally dissolved, the water whitened with all the fragments, mobile morsels, bitter bits. A fleet, hundreds of white pennants unfurled and fluttering. White for peace. G'wan now, drink it down!

Oh to be twenty years younger! You'd be a child again. That's what I mean. Shit! An intervention. If only we could stay on that tightrope from eight to nine in the morning, cross those waters running and violent like breaking waters on a morning of birth b-o, ba, b-a, bearing life out into 70° Fahrenheit and sanitized. 'Woman is a Nigger,' John Lennon here there everywhere in the multiple sounds of now including the dry deodorizing psst psst of a sponsor's message, or several, new and clean and plump. Esoteric side of the Québécois parallel, of what to note beside the litany of day-to-day, what muscular and day-to-day striations are embedded in the historic and geographic pumice stone of the region of Montréal.

## Four Times

He gets with the music, scandalously with love and hands. It filters through his batteries, tilts his remnant waverings like 'Gotta get to work.' Vibrations, ultimate undoing. Down his shoulders sneaks the beat, sound ripples round his neck, clings, then for the moment the cut lasts dies fragile shell inside his ear, bathes, moistens it in secrecy though all the world knows not the secret just the secrecy.

Music that pumps at the heart, distracts us narrators from Georges the textual character, stereophony full density volume and a-shake in seventh heaven 'She's a Rainbow.' Your lipstick will get what's coming to it Lucy Savage. Humming over the water rapid danger skims and my ears are perfectly in tune, exchange the modulated echo, to be synthesized – from the table a watchface emits a grandfather tick. Big Ben. Full blast. Georges imagines he's got rabbit ears growing from his temples, not outside but in, a predatory animal water lily in his soundwashed head, superbly sly too in his way of letting go when all's just right; duo / solo / trio. Exile / ejaculation. Triangular water lily 'associated with earth and water, vegetation and the world' of the underground.

Streaks of lightning sear his ear in symbiosis with the blood flow passing through, an act of the heart that stages a minor transient burlesque, livens the fete with colours such as to amaze a peacock at carnival time. Whiskey dances. Whiskey flows. Cascade.

A penchant for Lucy.

'*NIGHT CAP*'

THIS SNAKE PILL CAN SHOOT YOU STRAIGHT
TO HEAVEN FOR HEAVEN'S SAKE
PLEASE TAKE
WHILE YOU'RE AWAKE

daylight magnet common salt
gold and / or sun

Lo the delirious ear.

'Lao-Tzu had ears seven inches long.' Georges drops down a well, underwater where sounds are barely audible. Here reproduce by ear the zero point, the sexual clamour, the first coition. From audition to erection.

A pierced ear. A golden hoop fixed in flesh. Significant lobe. Violently Nick Mason perforates the ear / drum / skin, the rhythm explodes with nary a sign of weakening. Georges suddenly feels like a sleeper pearl at the tip of Lucy's ear, I see you, I'm into you honey bun, pearly dew about to drop.

I flow in Lucy, sweetly in her apartment. The corridor here's a labyrinth where fantasies fun rife like those crazy hammering sounds and senses from the amplifier like fire cutting out the world. Snip.

Cord.

Severance. But not completely.

Still awash in sonorous light. An epic of baroque baby blues disguised as obstinate rock with guitar lead like a genie sprung from Aladdin's lamp.

Take another puff reader chum.

The microscopic eye. Aerial view of the Island of Montréal. Marielle's purple Plymouth moves slowly now with other auto bodies on all sides, blue, black, white, purple; colour patches in the rising mist.

Oughta give Lucy a call. Have you got her number Alexandre? No reply. Lexa's still asleep. Oblong shape under the covers. Eiderdown. That reminds me … Music. I'll call later. My eyes are tired. Gotta make up my mind. I've made it up – no way I'm going to work. Bye-bye job. 'Being an ape's more exciting than being an accountant.' Hello King Kong, welcome to Colonial Street, an empire, a horizontal sexual Camelot.

## Five Times

Now the eyes turn aside. Enter a tradition, a written word, ancestors no narrator can be certain of. A nocturnal flora restless and underground like a nightspot at the height of pleasure. Each gets his share with Dionysus, sans exegesis. A shadowy troop crosses the marshy ground (a fictional fate) and gives a tipsy little tilt to surrealism and the gradual mutation from little no-good bums at ten bucks a job to slow-motion junkies at fifteen bucks a shot. Paradise at this time of night leaves one's back teeth clenched. Scary when the train goes by as well, through the back yard like.

Georges and Alexandre go wenching, do the rounds of cabarets, dives – holes-in-the-wall long since closed, filled in with cement, stone or paper board. Sharpen their barbs and go feliciting / soliciting round like pirouetting dolls and unsteered battery-driven tanks, attracting metaphoric bees and queens glowing infrared like the *lekou ne kiouffa*, women of the chase as they were called 'because they would give themselves to men returning from the woods.'

The Main was an era. Today it's down to Old Montréal, into history, through the written word and the retaliation it keeps producing for itself, for the pleasure of being seen, of being Siamese in shades of jade, of moving with readied claws. *Different* surfaces to be captured and recognized, the singular and strategic textures of a body and a place. Firewater, cannabis, descent to an enchanted world. Acid, plaster-mold trickster and magician, silk hat ready for a multiplication of loaves. Stoned. Dizzy, soaring above the herbage on the asphalt Champ de Mars. Flying saucers, don't walk so fast Alexandre, Nelson's Tavern's not going anywhere. But as for me, can't give you a better guarantee than to guarantee …

In Place Royale or the market place, a pilloried or gibbeted criminal (whoa back, can't keep up). In 1842 Charles Dickens came to Montréal (don't give a shit). Anne Lamarque Folleville ran a carabet (go on, go on) a cabaret in Montréal. She held her cabaret on a tight rein and often lovers round the neck and by the pecker. There was a long drawn-out trial in which they said she was a slut, a witch, an aborted woman and also (my italics) *a Venus flytrap*. Cut! Cut! That'll do, get me two more 50s. The spiel goes on, about the mopsies who were just too mopsy for the people's good and were branded with the letter M. The men got a pretty fleur de lys. M for Marielle. A sensation's impregnated in her flesh, a fist-clencher pain. On Elle's shoulder a mordant mark. Teeth, nails leave decorative imprints pink and red. Gently purple. Your legs, Marielle! Spread your legs. Marielle and Lexa, elastic fibres stretching and contracting all along their sibling ramifications. Inner playgrounds and active hands are in the game. Toadstool print on breasts.

It's so dark. So much can happen to our bodies. Which would you like, something real or fictional? Ground round at $1.50 a pound or the artificial red of cold meats on display, pigmented with temptation and comparisons? Raw flesh. Carnage. Etymological sequence and connection on this twelfth day of July 1689: 'Hauing entered the woodlands owned by les pavures de st-Joseph some four arptz on the Roade Leading to Lac st-Pierre Deponent was walking ahead of his Companion and was alerted seeing the vnderbrvsh broken To The Left of the roade to look and see if Something were in That Place Which hauing done He saw As seemed a bvndle of rags Owing to the twilight and Darknesse approaching, & hauing aduanced a little neerer to He saw the Sayd girl dead and Her Legges Apart and her Skirts Raised, And her face all In bloode And Lying on her backe.' Nicolas, Jeanne and Pétronille, brother and sisters, a genealogical trinity in the days of Neuve-France suspended above a textual void – characters bound by history to a parallel production.[1]

[1] The sight of the three children awakened the basest instincts in the walker. He overtook the youngest, Jeanne, who screamed fit to rend the air. She fought so vigorously that the rapist could not have his way with her. Furious, he seized her 'by The hand, Threw Her against a tree & Beat her with his fist. On Her right Ear ... '

It's so dark. Ride the Greek word *sarkos* till it breaks you in two. The word (lacking) in the flesh predicates desire. How has it been made flesh? On a boozy night in Old Montréal, between two fervent friends. In their very breathing.

The night goes by at an urban pace. The city has a shifty uncertain air with its artificial light. By analogy at this hour it's a city conceived in space, over land reborn bountiful, or floating over the seas. An arborescent structure of wishes, converging at the top, its fruits, as imagined, the abode of a brain composed of polyvalent and proliferating cells.

The night ferments, thickens inside the skull among all those sensory and motor zones. Makes one unfold one's wishes, form thoughts of going here or there, complete with itinerary or maybe none. In every way gives a yen for travel. Images and creation of some esoteric dance, or trance ——— of space.

The only way to return from night is slowly. Much inclined to gentleness.

Night. The city sprouts in Georges and Lexa like a mushroom. In their breasts geodesic domes protect them and filter love. A philtre before the dawn. The tentacular organ of death has stirred in them, henceforth resides calmly there like a thing of logic, an erection in stone.

## Six Times

Now it's flowing smooth and in the groove where a while ago it was pushing pulling inside and out. In the fog cars follow in grammar's wake behind Marielle. Maybe she feels she's a misfit on the main drag but if that's what she's thinking about she's out of character. Topless dancer. Hot-rod driver. Pin-up with hair dyed blue and frizzed up high, yes quite high. Bowling champion. East-end Point-aux-Trembles, place of trembling poplars. Falling trees. Candles and gutter. Broadway à la Montréal. An asphalt slash across the fields. Greasy spoons with tacky adsy signs. Gently the fog lifts. Forgotten now the ghosts and goblins but the white-coats from Saint-Jean-de-Dieu still lurk nearby. Nurses, n. masc. / fem. plur., anguish, banishment in the iron circle of their arms, old hopes and grievances relived in dreary monologue but maybe her imagination's working overtime again – who's to say whose eyes she's seeing with – word, words, s., plur. like a date to make and message to be got across with tip of hip I've seen her sitting on a toilet bowl a nurse wiping her rear and seeming to find it a tolerable pleasure to watch and realize the old crone's delight in defecating – *always, never* were the schoolmarm's words when talking of the damned. What are the major indicators of regression? That kind never run away. They sleep. They dream. They screw themselves lightbulb fashion to the ceiling. They give each other light, which lets us off the hook. Pervading sinister encapsuling Saint-Jean-de-Dieu. I dream of you – Jesus Christ will surely save our souls. Christ walks toward me like a Survenant, my version, a coureur des bois who comes and puts his prick in me on a barge. The river in a raging storm is my source. Flash, electric shocks – I'm no longer articulate. My subject's plying a route that cuts Montréal in two horizontally, follower of verdure and tall buildings, devourer of high heels and tires. Sherbrooke Street. Short circuits in quick succession. Red light, green light, yellow. Traffic light. Lucy's father, late, one autumn afternoon in a traffic accident. A short circuit, oblivion, a stop as if notched, if only time would stop but on and on we drive along and after a while don't even think about lights. Just drive with reddened eyes.

This morning Marielle *felt* her alarm bell sound inside but she finds verbs more satisfying in the present tense. Closer to reality Elle and Lexa. Colonial Street. This drive. The body's geography. The city takes on my maxims, my enlightenment.

Brakes hit hard.

Narrow squeak the black convertible ahead. A shadow in the scenery. Now forward move again as logical as lineal, no deviations or surprises. But marginally, on the feeder road, fantastic fictional impossible machines roar by, push on to broader arteries, concrete ones, perhaps to violence if there's collision. Ellipses crowd the meaning on every side, make it change direction like rain off a waterproof, reversible. Incursions of other words and vowels one by one trundle warily from one time belt to the next so beware of perturbation.

Exultant Elle with her bag of witty tricks.

So hotly used
Words get confused.

Camomille? Don't know her well enough to know if my narrator's going to use her to explore the currents underlying pleasure. I do know though there's a packet of illusions in the cards. Prestidigitation. In the palpebral fissure the crystalline lenses of readers' eyes are gestating a narrator and a use of tense and time. Wraiths and night-time haunts. Time to leave is always very late and rain's begun to fall. Chuckling rain down the sidewalk cracks.

## Seven Times

Early-morning opening of an eye. The crater-city's rim breaks the horizon as against a screen. The setting. Eyelids dark and heavy. The circulatory system's transgressing its appointed laws. The traffic too. Veinous, intravenous. Syringes and sirens, dual purpose for body and city both. Circulatory mechanism: blood slips easily along, moves as normally as a multiplier in an arithmetic table. October period. Settlement of account. Blood flows menstrual between thighs and spots the crotch of pants. Coagulates on curly hair. So what! Red and black like romantic literature. Hair, silky fuzz. Voluptuous fur as in days of yore on the shore of Hudson Bay when the hand that stroked beaver, fox, bear and wolf would kill stone dead to have a hide to tan.

Muscles in movement criss-cross scissor-like. This morning my whole body feels like a spinal cord, a spiky cluster of *rea*sonnance and formulae for making eyes react. Horizon (180°) like a forest at the limit of the line of sight, a throng both possible and impossible when thinking up a number to buzz near an ear, buzz the common measure where words are pronounced in sets to silence other sets of words, but are heard as static interference half-tone ho-o-o's sonorous bi-i-i's clearly devoid of cha-cha-charm, corn e e. Diffusion of the text complete with interference real and fictional: parasites. Creepy-crawly creatures – – – or bacteria (characters). Must feed on the text without destroying it. Bit by bit remove all its play (what's loose in it) and voids. With a pen-point fill it to the brim with pleasure.

Or if it falls by the wayside but rallies by dint of a broad sense of organization, empty it with systematic delirium, wave projections, a hypnagogic state. Reread the pleasures and rediscover the alphabet of sources to be conveyed.

Tendentious intoxicating Camomille. I open my eye cyclops in you, scour you from side to side, from one end to the other, giving imagination a voyeur's viewpoint – or an exhibitionist's. Bisexual perspectives – the Angels of Sodom in a detail, a glimpse as compelling as a stagey structure, a city shaped of fantasies behind the footlights; so permissive that masks drop and pleasure triggers faces and also beautiful sexual equipment as may be and sculptural to the hand, in the deep recesses of an opening, incestuous.

This morning I must feel awake, in broad daylight, with no curtain to protect or hide Camomille and Lucy's privacy. The blue of the sky makes me think of the tears of Eros / bookbound / that I saw in Lexa's room.

Red, I open my eyes: a state of mind. By day and by night a cirque ringed in red where centripetal and centrifugal forces make round Camomille and Lucy not just a motion of emotion but a vortex of desires: an ocean, 'a womb where death and life transmute one into the other.' And all of this hidden in the cubicled spaces of a tall insalubrious box wedged between two similar blocks, lethal cubes. Tall building / kakémono, translation for verticality with drifting shadows and junks mooring by the shore, early-morning fantasy, a membrane, hovering fog woven in silk. Ideogramme to be deciphered, blacks and whites on overtoasted toast.

Urban architecture reflected through the pupil. A rainbow toss of crystals from one tall building to another, long lustrous mirrors. Shafts of shimmering light. Forms circulating round oneself and also arguments in favour of silhouettes, shadow puppet theatre with less thread than a novel without a plot. Interference trrr, plays trick on trick like a ji-jiggling waterbed, a liido, crowded beach pigmentation through the pupil as re(a)d.

Looking very close you get an accurate impression of a 'wild explosion of photographic grain,' that's Camomille's face gazing quizzically through the window at the random happenings and distinguishable conflicts high drama playing out down there in the ravine, between those long concrete arms reaching down, or maybe up.

Lucy Savage explains: trouble is your heroes real or fictional are always men and if they're women they always end up thinking like males, producing as much, etc., etc. Variations on a double standard threaded in a spiral. Camomille, you stupefy me, woman. You get me stoned but good. 'Symbolic pollution' is something to talk about, I've heard. The kind of thing you just don't leave up in the air.

How 'bout going to Georges 'n' Lexa's? We could play checkers or chess or dominoes or noh, cook up a chicken or a storm of love. Knit, hammer, paint, paste, smoke or tinker … each getting off on his own thing, you listening? That's it! A word's emerging strong and clear. Camomille, how I'd love to stroke your breasts.

Fictional curtain.

Behind the fiction is a mirror, silvered glass, Camomille and Lucy in holograph projection, tridimensional faces on the curtain, a screen that reveals their pleasure, doesn't hide it in some shadowed fold, unthinkable circumstance.

Trickery and fiction through the body and the city. Feverish circulation of dark and bright red blood.

On the river's banks, like busy capillaries little old streets give passersby the look of gliding fibres, an unfamiliar air, a texture of parallel man on dancing axes, optical. Careful with that axe, Eugene. Red blood means arteries. From the heart of the city to the vital organs, to motivation's centre. All so I can pour forth for instance on a pregnant woman's belly, lunary flipflops, pour forth on and about 'vague sympathetic infiltrations.' Narrator (fem.), a circulatory mechanism in and through the order of words and titillating venues (murky little pun on Venus) filtered through to me or Lucy or another narrator,           , the way you infiltrate a rumour or follow (tail) an erected man.

Concentric writings (a Parisian urbanite can't get her breath for the pollution round her nose), writings concentrated on the lattice-work of parallels and perpendiculars. When I reflect that Camomille's thinking of 'a series of muscular protrusions in relief, the fleshy columns of the heart,' I long to write it to show how a woman's desire always seeks out forms in relief against which to move. From bottom to top – makes Colonial Street look horizontal the minute your image has to move to make an erectile empire state appear between King Kong's hairy thighs – the walls are active and vigorously.

Oof! This morning …

## Eight Times

Just past the municipal golf course, Sherbrooke Street veers toward the south. *Green space.* A zone where ozone's in the air like a sunny summer song. CKLM on the dial, initials, scheduled programs, why do they talk so much about waves no one feels. Marielle parks Violet on a sidestreet (could be Jeanne d'Arc, d'Orléans or Bourbonnière – further off would be too far to walk).

Botanical gardens and golf course next.

# NINE TIMES

Lexa had smoked and drunk a lot and woke the morning after feeling like a blob of papier maché...

and PASTY like a character in a true confections serial
5¢

Though he knew his hair was a mess, it felt Brylcream smooth and slick on his skull. well sleeked.

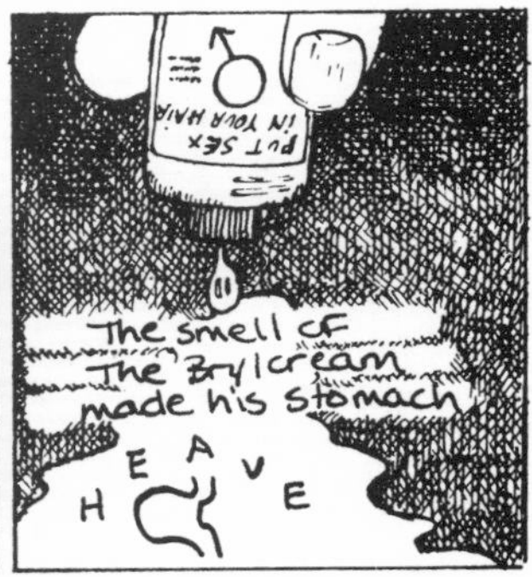
PUT SEX IN YOUR HAIR
The smell of the Brylcream made his stomach
H E A V E

up which skirts
in what atmosphere
would he go palpitate
offering his saucy cock?
?

NINE TIMES (II)
LEXA HAD DRUNK AND SMOKED A LOT AND WOKE THE MORNING AFTER FEELING LIKE A BLOB OF PAPIER MACHÉ...
AND PASTY LIKE A CHARACTER IN A TRUE CONFECTIONS SERIAL
X
X
THOUGH HE KNEW HIS HAIR WAS A MESS, IT FELT BRYLCREAM SMOOTH AND SLICK ON HIS SKULL. WELL SLEEKED.
THE
SMELL
OF THE
BRYLCREAM
MADE
HIS
STOMACH
HEAVE
ABC
UP WHICH SKIRTS
IN WHAT ATMOSPHERE
WOULD HE GO PALPITATE
OFFERING HIS SAUCY COCK?

Games. Children playing ball. Sound track that brings balls back on stream to my stream of thought, with slot or slit at eyelid height. Lexa, turn the page and dance for me. You're a cliché faggot, Alexandre. Platinum and jet. Louis XIV and Ming Dynasty. Frou-frou, boa, etcetera.

Text and illustration of those taunting pauses taken by Georges and Alexandre (before breakfast usually) after which they're on the go all day long mincing cheerfully amid the cars and trucks and asphalt tampers and power shovels and taxis and traffic cops and ambulances. Off to play outside with all those grownups. Like two live cells under a microscope, turning darting, queerly kite-like, play of lens and telescope. Like a pair of sponges, move through the crowd to a marengue beat, navels leech-like hungry and musical with pleasure.

Cock-and-bull Rocambole, sharp-eyed and obscene: 'The spaces in living tissue are filled with a gelatinous substance.' Fragile tissues adventure-bound, Georges and Alexandre wait patiently for a bus on Sherbrooke Street. It's raining buckets, wets (sic) the appetite. Water skates about the road. My urges this morning flap like ribbons on Camomille's tender brow. O for a soap scenario, good and bad playing good old blood and guts so there's no mistaking their saintliness and satanity. Rain puts strain on many a supposition, from the most prosaic (going to Murray's for a banana split) to the silliest (Marielle taking the whole length of Sherbrooke Street to swim to the other side, and once there all puffed out, finding the river where she needs scuba gear).

Waiting for the rain to stop or a bus to come, flip through a magazine. Tiny bus stop shelter. Heavy raindrops rattling on the roof, rolling off the black hump-back umbrellas brought out by the weather at this early hour when the vegetation, such as can be found, exudes vapours, fog and scotch mist that beads on cheeks 'cause waiting for a bus breeds furtive synthesis inside one's head, like a summary adventure that lasts no longer than the sound of a flock of wild ducks taking flight. Brown cloud above the treetops. Mouth-shaped the better to taste the water on the ducks' backs.

All that's as clear as mud! Get in, get in, we're wet enough already. What's our problem, Alexandre? Other people's problems, that's what. Bit too easy, isn't it? Sensibility impenitent at work.

The text moves like a small crustacean with compound eye and complex nervous system; throbbing, involuted, it becomes a parasite on a different body, animal, using 'filiform protrusions through which it sucks the vital juices of its host.'

Parasite or creature in mutation on the shore, *torrid* / delirium: mordant mortality, systematic competition the narrator against the I, leaking gas, a lapse of memory against a promise, an inset in a book.

A muscular, involuntary bulging in the breast, circling all its inner surface: mesoblast: *visceral.*

Rocambole, Arsène Lupin. Velvet and swirling cape.

*On the River*, fragment of a scroll (30 mm x 11.13 m). Ink on paper. We'll remember the water this tenth time, and the silks that emerged between the terms Louis XIV and Ming Dynasty. So unrolls the scroll.

Active limbs

parasites in mutation. We'll come back some other time to the subject of mounting competition and mortal mordancy.

## Eleven Times

Prospects in the setting. Coke-a-Lexa's heart finds harmony. Here the text groans like a rusty stomach. Amanita muscaria rises deadly in the underbrush – moss under the bed – pierces the bedspring, mattress, sheets – and Coke-a-Lexa's heart. Someone has said, 'Open a window in a fruit.' A quotation no doubt, spoken by that furtive voice shaped like a many-coloured coil. It bathes my ear, a gnawing echo while I enfold you Marielle, dear little older sister with your punchy pubic tuft. Montréal, this morning latent like the flu in a range of superficial terms. When Lexa's on a trip the stakes are double and no one quits. Coke-a-Lexa gives tit-for-tat in a modulated series of ticks and tocks. Tom ticks at a snuff of the stuff. Won't ever learn. Gets you down on a morning of pouring rain.

That's the way it goes. From one time to the next. Though you don't really know what happens in a city setting, behind the junk. In Lexa's or Camomille's private harmony. On the geographic map that shows all, streets, water courses, railway lines, clover leaves, etc. … a park and amusements.

Forest, mushrooms, beige domes radiant in the dew at daybreak. Lexa walks the line of a floorboard, a saucer balanced on an upright finger. Must generate constant transformation in and round myself vicinity Saint-James Street hard by Atwater supposing I transmogrify thereby but why? Because I haven't a clue what's what and everything seems paradisiac and magical. Maybe I've got bats as they put it in the belfry.

The earth rotates setator, heliotropic, coils umbilical about itself, loops like a hoop in an earlobe. You hang at the end of your noose, eternally asleep for one relative moment without pain, anaesthetized to just above your ears. Lexa stretches, lies full out in duo before the mirror at the foot of the bed.

The prospect's rosy – lungspace never used as yet. Montréal. 'Mademoiselle Mance (Jeanne that is) tolde me seueral tymes in recollection that along the shore for halfe a league and more one could see oneley meadowes spangeled with flowers of euery hue, which made a charmingly beauteous sighte.'

Then comes a sequence of situations and images bringing home the viva-city with which plants grow and quickly reach the heart and eye and ear. Stimulate. Then one's body is freed wherever it may be, flies will-o'-the-wisp in all directions in the mellow space of a morning filled with echoes.

Coasting through an echo, a thematic pleasure; a gay balloon aloft sporting with the winds. Breath. Spatial extension of the world. The I forgotten like a memory well-rehearsed and uncumbersome.

At this point you'd say that Lexa gives the narrators a funny look. As if inside his smile there's formed a sink-hole crammed with intimations, which however can't be grasped or fully filled. Textually Lexa's on the move. Makes a crossing, an oneiric trip. Toward ever longer mobile cycles, because there's light.

The bare lightbulb blinks positive and negative. Gives out Morse-coded information. The bedroom's pulse.

Relax, chum. The forked mandrake root looks like a little doll. Sleep, the mandrake will return you double what it's got from you.

. . . . . . . . . . . . . . . . . . . . . . . . . . . . . . . . . . . . . . . . . . . . . . . .

Snowflakes cool the scene. Sleep, but not complete. A state of hypovigil. With marvellous serenity, Lexa emits alpha waves (wish they could be seen), evidence of being somewhere else, in the deep repose of silence and of smiles.

## Twelve Times

Marielle alights from Violet. The sidewalk's not yet dry. Statistics yielding traffic data spring to her memory. Marielle, telephone receptionist in a highrise on Stanley Street. Always a smile from ear to ear in Inglish or in Franch. Today she's not just sick she's absent. Elle, inconsequential, eager and desire. On line. Really *up* on what's going on round her. 'Cept for Alexandre; she doesn't always dig what he's about. Isn't always consistent anyway, this little brother lost and found and lost again like a toothbrush that changes place and colour too just when you're about to use it *or put a hand on it* – there's a world of difference.

Traffic light red and flashing green. Flowers growing wild. But in the botanical gardens there'll be only tidy specimens, studied and detailed, bilingual information at the root. Great greenhouse. Venus flytrap. Exotic plants. Others, miscellaneous stems.

An infiltration via all the pores in the greenery, the vegetal carpet, mosses like circuits plugged into the trunks of trees, whorls – turn, turn, rococo, make the green shadows pivot round the orb of an eye, earth-like (paradise of verdure and fruits, complete with an Eve, like a rotting tooth made worse by all the hype – let's get it over with!); dance on the sundial with slow magnetic clock hand movements like a corny image of me coming closer and closer to you why not and now not later as you stroke my ears and antennae to quieten all the static sounds around us, all those darting insects (what fever, what delirium!) drawn by lush tropical plants. FOLLOW SOUTH. Images of snow assail my trail of thought: blank white landscapes of alienation, historical passages in a time-worn memory almost betrayed.

Foliage and shadows beneath arches of ebullient climbing vines as flexible as the necklet of coloured beans (dyed with acid red alcohol) that Alexandre wears night and day.

Marielle takes a rest where Nature is under control. Tempered. A thermostatic climate. Back to Violet soon. Just hope I got no ticket. Well, so what, all I gotta do's not pay. That's all.

A cat, a squirrel – a rare pair – scurry up … two different trees. Car door. Quivering exhaust pipe. Off along Sherbrooke Street. Destination city tour, like a tummy ache gone haywire in an itchy belly. It's beginning to rain again. Dirty raindrops on the windshield. I'd chance it with my eyes closed but since I'm narrating … (switch of tense: present indicator of the gray in the eye of the cat, the gray in the hair of the squirrel in the wood).

The retina registers: Red light on the horizon. Absent-minded pedestrians. Morsels of flesh, asses waggling some high some low. Bet they're OK types even if they don't know how to cross a street. Got no idea the risk from just one ROVING EYE. Eye for eye, tooth against cement; a car, living flesh folds, takes an unpremeditated shape. Body winded, swelled. Move along, move along! Smell of gas spilled under the car – a page hurtles ten feet above my head, as if Violet could have blown apart, flown fifteen feet in the air (might still). But how to get two such scattered things together, my text and that Plymouth driven by Elle? With ellevating ellusions, rhymes and mimes? Babullshit. Ellephantine acrobatics, aerial permutations.

Patter of rain outside the car.

## Thirteen Times

Could be five or six ways out. Put some heart in my gut. Probe the pleasure to be had in plural as in orgy and in singular as in privacy. Alone with a book and mastering seduction too. For all that comes into play, mastery and seduction. Ambiguities still good and wet and lubrified with taboos: transgression. Lucy Savage would hurl herself at the walls as the price of some outlandish image. Camomille's consciousness is transparent, yes – it that enough? Blue of the sky, topography, a rainbow's arc. Sky blue: haunting, tautological colour (in singular or plural) perceived or imagined like phosphorescent creatures that come out at twilight, zipped lip, mum's the word when crazy interdicted Lucy's watching you. Oral examinations. Word-jams in her throat. Log-drive on the river. Log-jams at the rapids. Shattered flying wood. Sounds of log booms through the atmosphere.

Transition. To fluorescence, undetermined ramifications. Into the labyrinth perhaps. Detours by the hundred the better to see the subject by. Lucy's progress is slow and gradual, to the point of taking on the colour and texture of whatever, whoever she's focusing on, metamorphosing to. A play of nuances. Lucy / Camomille, kohl and goopy eyelids, fluttering vibices … but you'd expect to see, imprinted on the retina in an opium haze, an image of Marielle stoned blind, her blue wigs, her woman-hole arabesques (as seen by ordinary folks whose cliché males are affectionate with whops in the chops), her candid shots of pleasure decomposed in such coarse grain on the paper it's hard to tell what the subject is: Camomille and Lucy making love like excited mermaids, sirens to some, double-takes, topless (voice) and bottomless (pit), membranes dilated beltline high, mouths open and kif-kif (inhale / exhale). Cloud.

Now a stab at narrative. The words change course, make another imprint on the retina. Become fixed, along with numbers and their acolyte unknowns, like raisins preserved for millennia in a

Cretan urn. Figs / females and pottery. Weight on the body. Sweat-producing work for shoulders and back. Burden borne on head, the impact and frequency of steps registered in jiggling breasts. All love's phases that find a body thus or so within a given moment; private trance and activated fine control of those waves that course through systems, nerves and muscles. Pure beauty – a flash entering the mouth, nourishment then cessation of sense.

Exposition of the situation: poses of women in repose, united in the art of satisfying their desires. Exploratory Aries / Sagittarius. Follow the moving waves in their brains to the highest point. Cautious astronautic navigation in their inner spheres.

Morning comes with traffic and gray daylight. Have to get up if we're going to Georges's place.

Suddenly up and in the middle of the room. Having slept how long? Made love? And having in the natural course encountered so many people, thoughts, images, sensations visualized, and having reproduced such private rhythms it hasn't yet sunk in how much has happened.

But there's a break in the recollection. Brief review: this morning Camomille and Lucy got out of bed and argued mildly while breakfasting. Then stood at the window and watched what was going on outside a while. Thought of giving Georges a call but loafed round finally back to bed and there made love. Then? A chink (fingernail play with the zipper on Camomille's jeans). Now to pry out, expose the reality / the fiction. So it was a pleasurable episode, OK, but what went on INSIDE THE SKULL? IN AND OUT LIKE BIRTH AND DEATH. Nothing to do with language. Happened neither in English nor in French. Not with words. With what? Something like a bridge in segments, a river-crossing with no retreat, heart in mouth. Memory blackout, wrecker of time between the narrator's ears.

Fibres of association should lead us finally to some plausible story or solution. But solution means water means the rest disappears. Total blank. Whatever can be seen that way? Unless a filter can be fitted in the story, to sift out static and clumps of cartilaginous words. Gristle.

Camomille, how about a little gym with Coutu on the tube? Only lasts a quarter of an hour. OK, I'm coming … Keeps you in shape. What else! Listen, if you haven't phoned Georges in ten minutes I'll organize my day without the rest of you. Yeah, yeah.

The sky is blue like my mother's eyes. This morning gray's OK.

## Fourteen Times

His slipper's gone haywire, crashes like a little racing car against the wall, turns turtle, motor roars, wheels a-spin. Violent. Alexandre counts the money he's got left how long will it last? A hundred and fifteen dollars and twenty-three cents to live on, beat, ruined like an old house huddled beneath Mount Royal's crusty flank, overshadowed by tall buildings and more going up.

Nothing left to do, to say, except recharge those batteries. Lexa's not going to be got down this way by a lousy gray Monday morning round ten too much in those hollow eyes taking it in where crow's feet converge you only notice them in noonday light – noon and plenty of rope to hang yourself with or follow to find your way back inside to work, the day's half gone and lunch hour's not really an hour. Bob-and-weave by a metonymic partial thing with no control of its story line. Alexandre makes progress with furtive words in a line of reasoning which must or should decide his course for him; here stop everything and get to know from bottom up the roots (gag the figures of speech and rhetoric), the signs of presence (for example, an erection at the sight of pigeons in Saint-Louis Square), the fervid incarnation of Marielle triumphant mounted on her high horse, in the bathtub (wouldn't say sorry for draining the hot water tank), uneloquently taking off for a world where nebulous words blossom over heads like parasols or cheerful mushroom domes.

Writing that feeds on zigs and zags and detours. Swallower / serpent. Isn't on every streetcorner but roams the streets, traces its course through them, as now when words bob up and clamour to inflate / deflate shapes and anecdotes. But most important is the narration of the inner odyssey in terms of Montréal's geography, its contours and harsh angles, sidestreets and lanes sharing the circulatory problems with the major arteries, from the heart of the city to the epicentre of oneself, the target and motive source.

You get inside the way you would some wayhire thing. You stay as long as your exploration takes.

First, decomposition of the streets, those familiar images beside the sidewalks; destruction of the language-power which controls the agglomeration. Segmented, percentiled in arresting quadrilaterals – hard to get out of once you're inside. The grammatical silt of imitation.

Imitation: fiction / reality. Whether to beat a retreat or stay and look it over carefully and at length. This is fiction but then I don't know what isn't any more. Fantasize a writing. Marielle drives along a Sherbrooke Street projected into space, an unsubstantial street, a fragile mental ground where first one word then another sprouts, forming images of introduction to a surrogate existence elicited by a fiction, or a reality: gives a yen for harmony, re-equilibrium in the laws of – what? Nature. A word is a potential sense.

Turn a die, a lie, ignorance, between your fingers. The realism of digits and a looking glass. Images and figures of speech. A copy of a copy, cold blades in contact with your wrist. The sense of touch as such. Feel sensation in a tactile effect produced by an image, a projection of waves of self in process of deployment outside one's usual arena of activity.

Henceforth phallin enters into the production of any text on pleasure and excitement. Principle at work and disarray in face of assault. Parasol, mushroom, dome. A game of chance. Mercurial. The mushroom, between parasol and dome, brings ecstasy, or delight in 'certainty of body'; in either case, it imposes first its venomous rule. Phalloidine.

Text at dead stop.

Then back to life.

Alexandre walks over to Aucoin's corner store. For cigarette papers and matches. To fire the powder keg and his hundred and fifteen dollars. Drop his twenty-three cents in a puddle. Fountain of youth. Pipe dream for an adult knocked and bumped from every side. Bumped, swung, dragged, hounded like a white elephant, a bilingual one and deaf to make matters worse.

The day is gray. Rotting wood. Peeling paint. The houses are slums.

## Fifteen Times

A private vale of shadows surrounds Camomille. Is madness really all there is on the surface, no comment, just undulating limbs seen through a window. Rather like blades of grass, white like those you see for example in the negatives of snapshots Lucy took on the Isle of Skiatos. Handwritten leaves, pine needles. Waving grasses that bend and straighten (can be held in a hand) and then again like arms waking to excitement.

Camomille stirs in herself, in her written body, the words and facets of anxiety. Hard to fathom, for we know so little about doubt and fear. Not being able to control her hands and arms, her gestures anymore helps her in a way prepare her sentences, pronounce her words, spell each syllable, turning into language all the urges that beckon and invite her to partake.

From one *time* to the next we go, recounting and weaving similitudes of ardour, fictionalized. Camomille Delphie flows strong in me like an affirmation. There's certainty and condemnation in the writing of a text, a cruise across and crossing of the senses and the sexes. Such as to necessitate a new formulation, a crossover, a transanimation of the body and its complex illuminations and secretory tournaments. Sweat aplenty for mopping up. The acrid drops evaporate on back, trunk, curve of breasts, as on a couple wringing wet, and drained.

## Sixteen Times

The traffic's heavy. Everything vehiculates. Everything circulates and animates space and time too when it's dead. Camomille's in fine form with forms visual and / or tactile to produce. Her imagination's at the gallop, riding astride grammar. Full gallop hell-bent for elation. Each moment widening her field of exploration, her experimental ground.

Vest energies, images, furies and fantasies in the orb of an eye, the lobe of an ear, inside a sensual mouth, and introduction to convulsion. Someone else's body in amorous trance, amorous deliverance from murky depths, a sensation which stirs inner bodies and brings them to the surface. Out of murky depths. Circulation underground but not abyssal deep.

At the peak of orgasm it's possible that Camomille hasn't moved at all. Possible that all has been illuminated, then disassembled like a fresco spread across the horizon's rim, carnal members heading in successive arabesques toward her sex. Would slip between those little lips like little ships, waters flowing fresh and normally.

In fiction / reality body and city get confused. The grammar of compound words. Copies and originals, negatives and prints. Casual air, air of love, and just plain air, but hot. Explosive. Grammatical ploys aired and henceforth scattered through the text, a logical and adverbial sequence which reaches into Camomille's recall.

So Georges rang Lucy to ask if they were coming this a.m. Since the hour's very early still there's time to do a lot of things. To the letter too.

Lucy dresses slowly. Doesn't rush. Takes her time in fact why can't others learn to do the same? Chest of drawers. Run into it kneebone average of four times every morning. Jeez. JeeZUS. Kneebone black 'n' blue. The blue of the sky in your eyes. You overdo it with your blue. Try sump'n else for a change. Easy: turquoise makes me think of jangley musical notes; indigo Django to a blues toon wafting round a steamboat, bluey cloud, en route paddling up the Mississippi. Going north of course, as far as possible, as far as home. Then what? Then it'd be like spinning you a yarn around a campfire, with mosquitos on the prowl and leaves rustling in the trees. And a peace pipe in my teeth. Peace inside. A long and absolutely unreliable yarn. Rank, verdant like the country in July. A tale of forests and (blue) lakes, rapids and broad, broad river.

We gonna take the métro? We'll see when we're outside. Gestures and forgets, thoughts and fantasies; the morning comes together bit by bit. The sun shows signs of showing. Has incalculable effects on the web of passersby in circulation, makes them swap their weapons for mirrors and disparate airs. A kind of white pale yellow sun gropes around behind the clouds. A hand hovering ready to pick a winning ticket from a huge white plastic tub. Getting close to pleasure, on the point of giving it. Sunny days are coming, really, but not yet. Puts a curve in the text, then another one. There's Lucy's nail bursting a suspicious superfluous cloud. To obtain an image. A sunburn effect. A mid-morning promenade on the esplanade.

You got a plan? No, we'll see. Depends. On whether Georges is in shape to talk, or we feel like a joint. Depends. Got a whole life ahead of us anyway. Lemme see …

We walk. Up and down streets full of grubby brats darting in and out among the cars so fast that drivers lose their marbles, mothers lose their voices, sometimes a brat his breath, or life.

Critical. Critical bent applied by Camomille to herself. Reflexion. While walking, a meditative phase. Lucy always wears long skirts. Today it's vexing because there are puddles still in the streets and pictures in the puddles, special effects screwed up as Lucy swishes by. Cuts short the pleasure on the retina, a surrealist woolgathering Andalusian dog cut abruptly, rudely from the scene. Marginal note. In an old old cinematographic shot in which no one would recognize Cherrier Street, or maybe it's a Spanish garden with some dancers – seems we've seen them before in some other movie, silent, or if we'd rather, whispering sweet nothings to their partners in the night.

In short there's a bit more than just the pleasure of walking down a street with a friend. The best of real and fictional scenes that we recall produce a pang, we've Lucy's word for it. A pang for the tango, electrifying legs and connected sexes. Cords in the heart (SOUL) and guitar lead, face to face.

Secondhand shop and season's giddiness. I'd like to buy me a grandfather clock. With beautiful gong incestuous bong at every half hour. Pussy cat.

## Seventeen Times

The text buckles with the thrust, the theoretic weight of risks to take, wind generators (glide, tame the urge to flee, take off in sheer abandon, ravishment, centre point of life vanishing vani … lovely spherical creature all pent up pulsation in the air – tame one's tremblings, form and sex equivocal when an airplane engine vrooms in the hum of a vibrator. Hear between one's eyelids (almost closed), parched mouth, parted lips large and small, wet and pressed *hap-ly* to the smooth vibrator shell, *rising panic*, rocket lift-off for the soul –), (wings for taking off, flippers for swimming above the city, its undulant vapours and smoke. Saucers and flying psychedelic forms turning red from acid layers. An OVERGROUND laboratory, refuge for nameless dancers as beautiful as intuitions of love and Grecian pastorals).

Layer, texture and overlapping as in the pauses Camomille and Lucy take while strolling down the street. A layer of words in very superficial word-word sequences like ice-floe – an active and animated overneath.

For the seventeenth time the text's attracting clumps of words, clusters, magnetic the way a field draws the flitting yellow butterflies of summer and also the architects who think up plans to make them disappear.

An urge for runaway narrative. Some oil.

Past Saint-Denis Street boutiques. Show windows and reflections. Camomille and Lucy walk arm in arm. Two pussycats from the roaring twenties, multicoloured scarves and berets pulled up / down over ears. Walk the way we once played hopscotch carefully not stepping on the cracks, the lines of grit and dust / every two / feet along / the sidewalk / unrolling before their feet like film, an uncontrollable sequence from a mid-length movie in black and white. Little candid camera shots of the street and verbal acrobatics to fill the empty spots – when Camomille stops to wonder whether this or that is worth wondering about. 'Cause there's a lot to take in, foot-support sandals and leather boots, sale signs, boutiques, beer bellies, tavern regulars with their forests of Labatts.

Postiche sentences.

All this written in the OVERGROUND laboratory and love for the parallel chemistries at work therein. The indicators: Alpha and Theta in freefall from above, our long hair swept up by a vertical draft. Message wires rising from each scalp. If everything were possible I'd say how much autumn is like a country village today. So (little dab of makeup, beauty spot).

Another sentence too about the seventeenth time, which we'd like to do all over again; all's analogy and comparison in this text, this interchange of attitudes and also tongues turning round and round in our mouths like spinning windmills, joyful impetus – makes you think of turnstiles you go through for admission to a show where what you get is latent images, expectation more than impression on the retina.

It's all a play of connections, illuminations and distress of letters fornicating before appearing not really clearly on the page. A detail deduced from indications. A fresco seen in detail and contemporary torrent too. A contrast in animation to convince Camomille. Eyewash to get me Delphie's attention and caresses. Shadowy Camomille singed by the sun, hotted up and thrust at me like a threatening profile caught in a flashlight beam. So I'm walking the same parallel as Marielle. A geographic and social route to be retraced. A symmetrical pattern of narration and the mutating characters which cast its lines of force, seen from the panoramic vantage point.

Postiche! Toupée or not toupée, aye there's the rub. The conceited ass thinks no one knows. A jerk with a smirk in the light of a feeble sun, the likes of an eclipse over Gaspé seen in Montréal. Far out and blank. Gives transparencies and evidence of epic fogs even in a city crammed with crackpots and all revved up. And for background sound, the rattle and ring of pinball machines, free games for the Minoan survivors of the urban labyrinth.

A postiche sentence so Montréal won't freak quite out to see itself mirrored in the river with all the historic garbage of outwitted, suckered pawns / / how long the text's been running on recycling its polluted swill. Discharge. Blank notes, an essential harmony. An affirmation in the shock of feeling death closing round oneself, and the text and successive etceteras like doubt and dread. (Well, I don't believe it. OK, suit yourself. It seems so natural. Yeah, seems. But that's no reason not to have realized it's a wig on the waiter in this place you wanted to bring me to for a beer at ten a.m. Wow, you're a killer-diller Camomille! Well anyway I'm getting practice, Lucy darling, luv. CHEERS, bottoms up!)

## Eighteen Times

Still a few drops of rain. It's stopping though. There's an accident in the left lane ahead. Everything's stopped. Marielle looks in the rearview mirror, deep into the eyes of the driver behind. He doesn't seem to have noticed. Maybe it's embarrassed him.

A theme for composition: Violet parked almost a whole wheel aboard the sidewalk. The sun begins to make a show on the chrome trim of the car. Sharpen those eyes. A comic-strip magician thrusting knives into incredulous flesh, his eyes darting fire and portents of doom. Penetrating. The little bit of sun's not strong enough to tell if there's a rainbow.

An accident en route. For example, if you look at the map it seems Sherbrooke Street bends south, toward the river. A little, not a lot. Signals a position shift, that soon we'll come to a part of town where brats and bums abound. Home ground to be explored. Comings and goings in strands of hair, in the back lanes of an ill-kempt neighbourhood. It fills the bill since there we see forms multiplied and motes are found in many eyes, grime – cinders no longer red. Red is in bricks like a linguistic colour in the mouths of children repeating things and comparing so that *same as* and *like* stick like wads to roofs of mouths then come out bubbles in the wind. Pop! In the end the words explode, stick to faces, make moustaches odoriferous roses under noses runny in winter and summer too. Got no time to stop and go eat their spaghetti. Pow-pow! Little tyke from Joliette Street, one day you won't want guns any more. See Ti-cul dodge across broad Sherbrooke Street to clean the windshields of immobilized cars. TIP, TIP. See how it cleans blgray rag. The scene blurs before the eyes of Elle, the lady with the blue-dyed hair. She's funny, eh!

## Nineteen Times

A fuzzy blur forms before Marielle's eyes. Gives them back the system of colours and shapes which seconds before were on parade for her. Pale transparent canvas and veil, washed-out originals when looked at from behind the dirty windshield of a car travelling at forty-five miles a how're. But there are traffic lights. So / a little while ago Elle pulled up at a motel. From the radio, words came suffering like burned toast about to be chucked, to vanish somewhere in space. There's no tomorrow for too much said. Hard-bitten words. Pointed things pressed against ribs a message to move. That was in the past. Our narrators have been wallowing in the imperfect past (lacking intuition) and it hasn't helped *relate* that 'certainty of body' *to the rest of the world*, to the universe, or the cosmos of the digit three / triangular expressions which they'll not have failed to flaunt.

You see, I was observing Marielle but was quite unable to describe her. There'd been a break somewhere. The static noise had gained a line of force, was putting out more sense than sound and ... marvellous it was to want, and win as when one gets over a temptation, surrounds it, espouses it in full dense rhythmic echo full inside the universe. Visceral flotation. I was observing Elle despite the interruption that will be taking place and surface at some point in the twentieth time. We wanted her for a character who, all being said and done, would end up profiled against a rubble of written contrasts and atmospheres.

Prepare the ground, hills and dales and flat. A crazy urge to put a quarter in the juke box and hear the Rolling Stones. Light up all the musical balls and those gaudy girlies, make them blink red green and yellow to the eye. Pinball machine and Orange Crush. Boxed up here cornice high, makes me thirst to dig with desire in the past. Archeologist and surprises in the subsoils brought to the textual surface. Turned over and aside perhaps like Camomille turning toward me and against me in so many twists and turns of love. Every day.

A text of daily life that loses us. No way now to balk or back away. Marielle will move through this book as she will along Sherbrooke Street. Horizontally, on an open map of the city – spread out on the desk with the corners curled up like the thoughts of a crafty fox plotting a theft of tender young hens. Mittened paws trampling the verdure of the text. Fragmented, a scruple to subdue over depicting the bodies that give life to the city, the dissimilarity of bodies, epidermis / texture, radar and decoding of waves. Shooting stars everywhere. Harmony under heaven's dome. Celestial.

Bodies: tonic cells, systems and mutation. The city dilates, contracts, the challenge of perceptions lends itself to the ear like a whisper destined to bring forth moments – who knows, some day when death's abolished, its very name may never more be brought to mind by rows of posies, oxalis, radiant with fleshy bulbs, flying pollen, spread by word of mouth like the scriptures of antiquity

and symbols made flesh in new dexterity, reflections stepping from the mirror water, waste and potable.

The trees sway but she tells herself it's the leaves and puffs a laugh. Leaving the …… Motel, she steps on the gas heading for the next. Violet attracts as much attention as a politician's Cadillac, or a limo with a mafioso, a BIG BOSS in the back seat fingers wrapped in three four diamond rings. Motif: an eight-year-old car. Driven by a woman with blue hair. Whets the imagination pop / poppop / pop the clutch is shot ba-a / ba / ba / bip don't give a shit.

## Twenty Times

Text that goes on and on. Intervention of matter which composes and disposes, is there then gone like a gloss on the architecture, or plan. As for the inner discourse, it's a pencil poised – held by a hand that temporarily appropriates its sense and manipulates it like a juicy victim hanging from the speaker's lips – a system of pain and pleasure, of exhausting circumstance, more deadly than a night without sleep.

The sense of night. A night that belongs to Camomille like the joy in her belly at being her own lover and her body's, tender ecstasies that swell and cause to swell beneath her skin like young unfolding ferns. Green herbaceous life inside her body while all around is revelry. At every turn we'll recognize ourselves. To be continued: words, whirling helicopters, throbbing convictions.

Camomille. Zone and crossing. Subterranean passage. LET LIVE OR DIE. A picnic of love and fun. It's begun and keeps pouring out: lapses, ground swells, springs, sperm, ludic tics, ochre and autumn put to fire and sword in vision's veins.

I love you Lexa thinks Marielle as she stops her car, purple grin and laugh unleashed. Gee, what luck. A fuzzy blur of characters. List of words to choose from. Lexa, double saliva and spelling that lends itself to touches allover moreover. Snickering she.

## Just Once

In which the text slows down in Camomille's mouth, salivating letters and words of love the better to … suck on fragments of fiction. With all the energy of irrigations and convergences. Membranes that meet and meet some more till the last contractions, to exhaustion. The ultimate dilation. Ecstatic perfusion in Camomille's mouth. An exile throughout the long lingual journey over those plausible surfaces and mucous membranes connexting in her mouth. As if in a muffled world filled with liquid symptoms, concentric desires, capsules within to be opened and discovered, little scaly pink fish of that 'miraculous catch' whose stirring and harmonious lilt we feel in the merest reflex. Lick at those walls. Prolong the desires with the telling, the narration of a long uninterrupted kiss. How hard it is to articulate or devise compromise. The kiss, a ball of fire. Life's serum restored with undulant and penetrating movement, a reliving of the taste and smell of birth for a tongue consumed in dance beneath Camomille's palatal dome, Camomille whom I love with all my power of intervention. A wish: to abolish walls between mouths. Mm-mmm the taste of it.

Luckily keeps flowing in the text and on my tongue, erotic substitutes, and luckily that tipsy feeling in the dark, inside beside a cheek so just enjoy, rejoice in the juice, turn and return to that first excitement. What is excitement? Encouragement to do what you feel like doing when seen by someone else / the reader in company with Lucy, Georges or Alexandre, or Elle; being used to spinning out one's dreams by muddling one's own reflection in the mirror so marvellously that paradoxes come to life and whatever the cost force a retake of the sentences, the caresses that started the excitement (what did we say it was?), stimulated spine and breasts dandled in a hand, a phallus emerged invitation to oblivion, to the feel of rhythmic shudder, loins more titillating than some corny happy-ever-after tale, pelvic basins the pornographic mudholes of one's imagination. Narrator fem. / masc. Pelvic basins liquid base. Stop and ruminate a moment near the pond, the basin in Lafontaine Park with its little boats going just fast enough to the music of the band on a Sunday made for sunning in a park with sunning playing fountains. The water basin changes shape to triangle or rectangle. Like imagining Versailles made avant-garde. But how old and worn the film, how grotesque, like some faded foreign boulevardier … then, as if from one exploration to the next, a long hop to Chambly Basin, immersion there in unmuddied waters fed by springs, our origins, a running brook of words rippling-aroused tracing a thigh-line like a hand, retracing the story line the better to write it down. From that point on it's ink and blotter and quill by power of suggestion. Confusion springs.

Again, Camomille, your mouth, that's good, you get me off!

When the text lets Lucy move, we'll make her arms stir just barely round him / her, her partner, for Lucy's seductiveness is bounded only by the italics in a sentence and italics become her like any pleasurable and prettifying artifice, disguising her almost. So seeing them together we, in the guise of narrator, end up flitting deliciously from one image of them half naked to the next as in some threatening text, brandishing blackmail photos before pale frightened eyes, above a man undone, stuck dumb – a movie *Caligari* lurking round the background. And those corridors. Tongues slipping through. Chew in ardour and get chewed. Reptiles about to shed a too tight skin. Mimes of fiction in the tender realm of Camomille's mouth and mine, I reaching for the limit of how / where to pass beyond and leave you to whatever, Camomille, or persuade you to cross with Lucy to pleasure's realms, with Georges to pleasure's realms.

The moment of the kiss comes at the moment traffic sounds cross Saint-Denis Street from one side to the other, on the heels of pedestrians, getting stuck between the wheels of buses, caught like a sound in an ear in a baseball glove. Traffic / circulation in the heartbeat's private mutterings. *Lakes* had taken shape in Camomille's eyes I recall – though her lids were closed – hunting and fishing lakes in spring at dawn when the mists don't rise, don't rise even for eyes asleep and gently moving, shadowy reflections of signs left over from the night before, and spun of dreams, sufferings, self-completion when the body's smit with lovely images, in fluid mood.

Camomille, it's good inside your mouth. You (I) send me bats completely bats.

CRACKPOT. Carnival mood. Twentieth century the way I like it. Vibes, brainwaves yow-wow-wow which … listen … Begin again: on Camomille's lips a kiss, rather chaste. Nibbled lips. Pain / relaxation. Pleasure, lips licked, left wet. I slip through the slot the text provides and enter Lucy's homosexual fantasies, seductive Lucy in total control of herself. The slot, parted lips, saliva. Like victims in a racy murder mystery, the membranes yield oh so gently to my tongue probing deeper DEEPER INTO THEM. OOF.

Shudders and muffled sound. In the city ramifications undulate on no specific course but round construction sites. Geography of reliefs, tongue against your teeth, in cheek, tickles hee hee – comes on like an electric train or a loving toothbrush jiggling with joy, rubbing, tickling gums – those gaping holes downtown, sprawling ranks of cars parked all humpy rounded bumps. The city in relief beyond the moment of right na-ow. Visionary and vulnerable – emerging from the Hippolyte Lafontaine Tunnel eyes blinking harder than those far-off yellow lights. Emerging from an analogy as from the analogy of tunnel and urethra, along a long straight line. Canal / communication. Oil on the tarmac, a few reflections on the surface of the road. The moment of the kiss, you realize, coincides with Marielle's arrival at Saint-Denis Street, where she enters a busy bar-restaurant, crowd ahum and rhythmic, panting and expectant.

There fiction takes on / loses all its sense. Let it melt into what's real – there's not much sense to any of this if not *this* pleasure, *this* sense, I mean to say this play inside a mouth which, apart from choking her, offers her a thousand ways of composing pleasure on a tongue.

She spots her brother, Lexa dahling. Melts in his arms, that old delicious fantasy. He lights a joint for her. All's serenity while David Bowie beats his breast, with rhythm to the rafters and round the chairs, revelry in the smoke as it escapes and circulates like a French kiss urge. Camomille's left leg pressed against Lucy's.

The right one sweet against Georges's.

People coming in and others going / passing out: a minor neighbourhood event. The barroom door keeps swinging like a body wavering between two river banks, rivals.

Five around a nondescript table. Surface and smear of beer. Ashes. Insufficiently appreciated posters take revenge on eyes. Colours explode on retinas, corneas pop. Puffed-up bags. Uncontrollable bags and pipes, music, organ-word resemblance – stare very openly past Alexandre's knees, inside his BVDs. Detached we float above the tables, evidences dangling in mirth. Taste of peppers and pepperoni. Camomille eats a bit of everything, tastes everything when mouths open and breaths crisscross, exchange. Breath. Bit of chicken stuck in your teeth? What you been eating anyway? Oh, never mind! Into your mouth with my tongue, teasing like a lure to a fish to make you come. A fish swimming with the sperm's current, a pouring sweat of panicky words as the page turns laboured breathing. Must make sure the phantasms get to us from over the horizon. In the slippery occidental night whose existence Lucy's trying to deny. Abort the premonitory signs of fear. Realize that the city won't ever be reproduced to suit privileged eyes and ears like ours plugged into all forbidden things.

Lucy and Camomille drift with the music from cut to cut, side 1 the funny side, side 2 the head-spinner of the platter, drift at the speed of the water's flow and ... the bed's a vast surface where birds come pecking in the sere of autumn. Dead fish.

The *language of the birds* speaks for itself. The 'verbal alchemy' of analogies and phonetic equivalents. A prayer of joy heard through the other's wisdom teeth, whence, with saliva, flow into Camomille powerful intuitions of movement perpetual and circular – around gyrating hips and waist hoola-hoop on the sidewalk after supper before dark, try again, can't do it, how you ever going to learn to dance? – inclusive hoop.

Each mouth leaves its colour its copy on the other. Each endures the other like a wintry cold, lips trapped in ice. Exceeds its bounds, a circus of two, two educated animals alone occupying sweetly all the surfaces of desire. The tongue's like a cutting word, a flicking whip, Camomille, arch your tongue – the way you do your back – a whip that flicks until it bites your tender flesh. My sanity's a hemisphere.

Words get confused
so hotly used
phonemes
celebration

The language of the birds speaks for itself

and what follows flows saliva lips scars spoken aloud over which to linger a long expectant moment, to dream as it were or to make mirrors talk back to us, ambiguously and resonating on our eardrums. The city, the fragile clink of glasses raised then put down on tables. The curious lapping sound of tongues before they find each other in the dark spaces over Adam's apples that bob as if in warning. Mouths touch and salivate beyond control, venture blindly toward each other. Toward the dark. Each to lose itself inside the other's geography. Camomille regains her breath, the other's breath, its difference marking her deeper than the fingernail she's digging into Georges's arm. An assault by a ramifying thing irradiating all its surface, epidermis – her desire.

Her tongue folds, unfolds, folds again, sucks at the other tongue, triggers, lubricious and circumstantial metamorphosis under the palate's / palace dome – under the verandah, pull down your pants, I won't tell (gustatory memory: popsicles, pink jujubes, popcorn, licorice, tootsie rolls, rock chocolate, peanuts) – like a deposed queen, her tongue yields to the other weakly with tenderness, disengages, drifts, a multiform body sought. On a wave of vagueness.

A detail on vagueness: Camomille agrees to make mirrors and shadows and incongruous details talk. Nuclear love. Brings a lump to my throat. Almost makes me think I'll always love you. Time to catch anoth-other breath.

This morning everything was wet. Sometimes I think I'm sinking inside you. Downtime for Camomille.

bullet bitten, bit in teeth, she squints and her eyes itemize, recompose like a kaleidoscope, detail by detail, one petal at a time, one shape and then another, a text of successive surprises; a city where lanes become streets. Elle in a nutshell, animated by all possible pulsations, varying the spaces, invention at play. Emcee for herself and for lines of force – prospects in mouths duplicated – a tracing.

Now to put her tongue in the other's mouth. Her desire in the city and geography. The other's house / garden path.

The city revives in their breath, their speech; perks up a bit. Because of names of buildings they must drop, streets they used to take to get to work, smells they discover to have clung to their hair during the day. Georges obliges, lifting a lock of hair to his nose. Asks Lucy too to bear witness to those curious and many smells that stick to a scalp any day of the week. Almost a demonstration; wild enthusiasm (suddenly) for the smells of other people's hair. May go over by a hair's breadth if hair's not one's bag. Alexandre extends his train of thought as far as the station whence he walked to Marielle's one day. The city emerged at the moment he did from the Queen Elizabeth (Station Exit) and, polluted, grafted onto him. Profiles of men and buildings. The streets ramify anonymous, juxtaposed, and bring him back to now.

His / her tongue in the other's mouth, a subterranean passage where / during which he / she slips some information by body language to the other, a narrator burdened with decisions, optical letters in colour; two ends to choose and make meet in the text – let doubt take over, narrator (fem.) astonished by Camomille's transparency, her real facial / fictional traits, fleeting as when one loses oneself or maybe the other when making critical decisions from which one really doesn't hope to gain a thing, just store away each smile and each caress. At times of loss we dare to wish death on things. Flow and let flow like self-destructing ink over pages and pages of entreaty. Object: to exert loss of control over whoever / whatever and wherever on the globe. Ocular exertion / reading. The dimensions lost in the assembly line. The object decomposes. Forbidden zone of decomposition / decomperdition. *You the deaf,* look to your ears! Perdition. The tongues get hungrier, leechlike, draw bigger huffs and puffs. One stronger puff fired red-hot to bring forth amorous penchants for other inclinations. An oblique tongue, silent like a detail. Which suddenly I like.

Friday squeezed between one's legs like an animal that won't calm down. Near excess. Teeth and nails unrestrained the better to gnaw through the tie that binds, that holds back the body's shudderings, joyous rhythms gr / um / p 1, such endearing ways; upside-down syringes in our heads. Not battered but disoriented heads, *wingover weather vane, I learn from all this as always what's best and what's not so bad in our forbidden bents cocking snooks toward the north.*

Ramified belly and text. Coincidence. Georges tilts and rocks his chair.

On Fridays all cats are gray.
Marielle's back from Lanoraie.
Another week begins.
Pim(p)s at the bar.
First choice.
Bully boys with sidewhiskers.
Bread and dough.
Dark décor in purples.
Traffic around the tables.

Movie house: moustache, black and white on May Irwin's white upper lip; one's first kiss which wasn't quite, a PECK almost but not exactly on the mouth.

unbutton the text and prod it to get rid of inhibitions in a narrator who changes them to make them fit a personal desire for prolonging pleasure, keeping a few forbidden things, a few mad impulses; when bodies are to be disguised, convey their attitude with lots of lascivious posturing.

Friday like an animal to grab by the scruff.

move along the circumstance, the other's lips while tongues travel each seeking to suppress, annihilate the other from a vantage point of mastery when one yields, gives ground, salivates beyond control, gives up its energy to the other whose power of domination it becomes.

upside-down syringes in our heads squirting dense dramatic scenes and fantasies upward to the sky into the blue. Disconnected speech, the world upside down in our veins, adrift ... incense-perfumed super super neurons injecting upward, high above our heads and higher still, images of strange wild beasts astride other beasts galloping, galloping unrestrained, suspended like undecided meanings beyond the blue, super she-monsters, witches, Corriveaus uncaged assuaged in the gray of cumulous.

on Fridays cats chase round the neighbourhood lanes, through yards where little girls play with dolls to pass the time, like that old aborted dream of trucks and planes you can play with and get away with. As for dreams, even pimps once believed in them. Anyway with so much talk those dreams got to sound like fairy tales, bedtime stories for putting us to sleep ... once upon a time ... story cut short. Brutally by a speedy bouncer. Lost his head and fired into the pack, finished off the lot almost. Orgiastic violence.

catapults syringes cats and little girls so long long ago don't remember nuttin' no more nohow nowhere. Collective loss. Blank sleepless night and GUNS not loaded up enough. Blank, blur, ble, back to childhood (October 30,1973).

## FRENCH KISS

On with the kiss, so dense it strangulates articulations; pleasure moans. Weep talk laugh pleasure suffocates and makes tears well up in eyes and trickle back down over rounded cheeks. Lucy undulant amoeba, a fellow traveller cell while crossing arid desert zones. Remote seductress, imbibed in the text and gentle curves of love, she gazes round her, faraway like a Garbo idolatrized, makes heads turn. Fix on her. A mixture of words mixed with sensations. Real forms – a tourniquet.

Fix my lips like leeches onto yours, a sense to be got across to you. An Iroquois dream: lipstick, the other's dancing teeth, tongue around a red-hot cold sore – hurts! Firm tip of tongue (as in a picture in a doctor's waiting room), forked diabolical tongue of a torturer drawing near his victim, thirst aflame.

At this point we'll have made lines, nerves and avenues cross, retraced the broad outline and motifs. But let's cut out the trite intrigues.

Imprint of fleshy lips on other lips in footloose festive mood. The city. Beat-up lanes and snack bar at the corner; display Camomille's lips and desire as urgent functions to fulfill; a level crossing bristling with risks and danger of getting stuck … of not being able to move along to town, to the red-hot resources of a zone seething, bursting with activity, exhausting.

Mordant thought.

Ramify all inclinations till the sense and fleshy parts and functions are transformed. Turn on the spotlights to set the scene. In the darkened hall, the silent kiss is seen on the silent screen ——— FRENCH KISS, lapping sounds, the kiss as bite on film, nuns and vampires, *Nazarin, Mourir de plaisir*. You see, Camomille, taking my time this way, my teeth forget themselves against your neck, feel like priceless smuggled diamonds. My delinquency.

Felonious narrator, mutterings, dark seething waters and every imaginable succession of words. An un / lashing of ties / to get our teeth in / to / as well as grasses and jackasses amid the city's density. Population – Papa see the traps open and close, rise, flood the scene. Fog, smog. Rot and ruins.

Noisily, Georges stirs words and things in his head. Pulling objects behind him on the floor, like interdictions. Inter / dict, int / eradicate the words in speech, unsew their fabrics, pantsleg hems, having one's highwaters on feeds the millrace of desire. Room for everyone.

Morning firewater, sorta. Behind the curtain, the rain puts strain on sentences. Parasitic words under one's tongue, and jawbone moving curiously.

A raccoon raid on the narrator's apple orchard. Apple peels inspire a smooth tenderness that's effective on your belly. The softness of teddy bears and love.

All of which just gets the lips apart, gaping like hungry traps inviting flies into the ink, there to sleep and sleep some more while I get back to the         text and Camomille's lips.

Concentration on / under the roof of the other's mouth, a moving staircase escalating toward the dark, the uvula, and the phrase *palat(i)al roof and gardens*. Poetically falling rain. Rain, city, ——— spiral stairways on Saint-Denis Street; and the roofs – roofs are over heads and minds, control of consciousness, soon brings an urge 'to escape from our individual consciousness, break up and out through the roof of a mouth or house.' Transmutation in mouths. One struggles without voice to forge a voice the way a wrought-iron balcony suddenly gives access to the city's far-off sounds when you step out round midnight to breathe the air and stymie sleep awhile.

Essentially, the exploratory fabric woven from your characters' saliva takes the turn determined by a concentration of energy which you let explode at ir or regular intervals.

We know beforehand that the kiss must end. As surely as the population density diminishes once Marielle has crossed the intersection of Sherbrooke and Bleury Streets. The kiss can't cover the whole city. It's bound to the ghettos of our mouths. Same way love was bound when I wrote *perhaps forever* speaking of nuclear love in a dialectic of possession. A code and palpitation's trap.

Camomille *brushes on strategy*, with curling tongue and penetrating movements in the other's mouth. Funnel shape and spiral. Water-fall, fall of bodies.

It's getting dense and hot because people are coming in in droves for the lunchtime special spaghetti and beer. The shady morning guys have gone. Now it's ordinary people we're being jostled by. Terribly like boredom.

A glass of water, tomato juice. A MOLY. Camomille is still several intuitions ahead of Georges and Alexandre. In her forced imagination they laugh like shutters flapping against a wall 'be-cuz be-cuz' of a wind which always bears off something of the images behind them to areas of so-so ambiance, like vacant lots. Mucky spaces, li'l tin cans, ol' tin lizzies, everybody's discarded fridge. Coke-bottle view of the horizon. Green shards not sward. Yellow autumn grass. Rain, rain. A glass of water.

Elle and Lexa talk in stage whispers, cheek to cheek – prelude to a tango of licentious love, brother, sister dear – tenderness. A *mother*ly *Mary*Elle for the nonce.

Sketches, plans. Maps of the city, abstract but also real. Asphalt and billboards. Destroy all solid, tangible things, build crazy objects, towering and scary ones like suicides.

Mother, my tongue's hooked on your snares. Lexa's gambled and is terrified. I tell you mother, all this stuff about contractions, *expulsion* and desire's like wheels spinning in nothing, we're in the age of mutation. Incisors in your hide betide … Why can't she take our liquid discharges, once and for all! Complete the cycle (tri) / (try). Descent of bodies in a ring; gold, sun, orbit. Then disappear over the horizon like an orange. An odyssey.

Two MOLYs. The bubbly brew sticks blond to Georges's mustachios.

Lick at the sides, suck at the bits of food dangling from between the teeth – tendrils of celery, vines for dauntless Tarzans to swing by, by and by – transverse line of the tongue like a fiddlestick drawn across the strings, vocal cords by which you can hang with the ponderance of all those muscles and of fountain water playing over music playing in a park, hang from her neck like a sapphic semantic charm, taut like a lesson; pressure on the larynx, strong medicine that constricts your memory and wind. One capsule, one tight encirclement.

And yet, Camomille, all this proof that your mouth gets to me gets me.

Runs over my whole body like a car or truck travelling along Sherbrooke Street past rooms to rent and paunchy bombé wrought-iron balconies. And beyond. Through a fuzzy fleece of lanes, busy blocks of busybodies, back fences and clotheslines – Cree creepers for swinging across pitfalls from one side / from the other, playing Indians, growing up aware and passionate.

Georges draws away from Camomille but soon is back, enticed. It's as though the kiss is riddled through from stem to stern with *flying laughs*. Laugh. And stalk your words, slipping in and out between your teeth, wind on the rise, that old signal warning you of bursts of laughter. Fragments. You'll hunch your shoulders, bend your head the better to find them, read them, hidden points, darts leaping to darting eyes, moving targets.

Fragments plastered against your gums. Write at least to make your mouth open and close. On silence. Once it did on sleep, I recall. Open the space up wide inside but don't rush – water, rain, saliva.

Threads of drool stretch from word to word, spread ramiflorous inside / outside your throat / your lips. On the verge. The sentence is undone, dishevelled like a trumped-up tired old film effect showing a woman. Just having come.

And this recalls a certain 'neurological fidelity' between Camomille and Lucy, between couples and this three-cornered, two-faced text. As though, without realizing, both characters and narrators had dropped their masks, plunging on despite the risk of surfacing in historical or future baroque style; undone and re-done by an oblique, penetrating laser that leaves us where its beam has been, heads bent, suppliant.

Between Camomille and Lucy and … Marielle, the city and its structure. A concrete jungle in which a writing looks for cracks and openings, telltale breaths of air, hoping for a passage through. If writing dies, so will the city and its harlots. Will wrap about itself like a grieving young widow's luxuriant neurosis. A microscopic serpent in the testicles of steel contracting males, stainless to be sure. Rouses then goes all soft again … to which one doesn't feel like reacting anymore.

Montréal transpires; a sweaty sign, proof to be worked out, that your desires are not my realities. Your mouth open to mine. Heresy. Breath of both compressed. Breathed in. Lower belly twitches like moist felt wings aflutter. Must drop anchor. Then sling some ink, take off with palpitating pen. Lucy's tongue turns like a wild propeller in Georges's mouth, clips electric snips from the blue of others' eyes, crammed with cross-references. For signals. To set my mouth in motion against yours. Get to the point of a tongue. Head off those symptoms that make you tighten up, pick out semantic fields that are booby trapped – pressure of a finger on a … blackhead. Black on surface, blank in sense. Put teeth in the sense of a vertical desire. Bared. Bare flesh and decomposing word for word in the sense that's lost.

Eager, perspicacious Camomille.

'Man locks himself in his own eye.' Alone decides to be born, to take that wild turn one does when possessed by the optical illusions one pins to reality.

*Fiction.*

The inside of the bar-restaurant begins to feel like a uterus. The rush hour's over and the customers who stay stay because it's warm and comfy there, on no account allowing the alcohol count in them to drop. Cheerfully shadows take on shapes, busy movements, stick together in the semi-dark, stand out like beauty spots, fine figures, dark baroque gems unperiwigged. Jawing to beat the band. Just now it's fat thighs and cellulite. Flabby stomachs. Paunches and heart attacks. Each a gray manner of airing the matter. Feces, farces, phrases, bile and aching head ————

———— Montréal by feel, forward, back, upright or crouched, Montréal fractured on its east-end surface of cultural crap. A crack across. The balconies crack and rot. The body's anatomy suddenly resolves into another, the urban anatomy of layouts and corridors. Tattoo on its skull, *no* entry, parking, U-turn, left turn, right. With illustrations of the right way to proceed.

Ramifications and contractile profanities. Inspiration / expiration. The lungs' alveoli move, suck in air. In the breast an appetite for life swells, puffs up, tortures desires. Then decomposes, seeping creature smells intriguing to the nose. Which reacts. Result: in the breast, the architecture dallies mid blissful scenery. But the cement is cracking and the rest keeps seeping as though secretion instinctively begets rebellion. Demerits like a dose of radiation.

Train my narrative intentions directly on your questions. Wait.

Slow myself down.

Bum around the neighbourhood. Watch one's time by one's watch. Bluff, hang loose and jocular. A crazy way to levitate . . . . . . . . . . . . . . . . . . . . . . . . . . . . . . . . . . . . . . . . . . . . above the city, a huge map with dotted lines from edge to edge. Islandwise. Collage-montage of neighbourhoods in jigsaw puzzles round the mountain. Suckling through the soles of one's feet from the vegetation, water ... *current* ...

At the island's tip, bridges like deletions for cutting in the text. Trace clear-cut autoroutes with maniacal cloverleaves full of twists ... in your mouth, seven tongue twists before speaking, to say exactly what? To say one doesn't want to talk at all. Camomille comes loose in the kiss like a sentence in your mouth that's tried too long to take a pause. And destroys itself. Other sentences get lost. Some get into books. Sentences a mouth spits out, parasites on its membranes, bugs killing themselves with green relish. From your mouth to mine, having a ball and all. Touching, exploring you, disseminating me. Textually so.

Thing is that part of the body might come loose and take off on the wind, like dust / depart. So in a zone once well defined which threatens to come loose at every other line, improvise. Space for discourse.

The time for checking things out comes after the words have rarified.

I'm not confusing things, I haven't even pressed the manic button, the right one for fishy sides and metal rods and coloured spellings on lighted billboards along the Metropolitan Boulevard. Tigers in tanks. I turn on and over the traffic conditions, about the possible potlatch on the blank page. String come undone, necklace of teeth falling, fall, fa, f. Low gear in your mouth, finger poked all the way to your Adam's apple. Heaps of cheek.

no limit no way on the sentences being turned          mouth (fragile paper tiger mouth) spaced out jagged crack          an opening to
make you talk lick you like an asshole improvise around an anus

I'm not confusing things.
Lipstick. Vaseline.

Shiny table surface. Alexandre bends his head a touch. Concentrates on a smear of spaghetti sauce. Scratches with a fingernail, graphicks graffiti in the texture.

Sponge, wipe, water. Pores / arborite. Absorb the liquid. Drink like a fish out of water, in a vital space, a void. Not a water hole an empty hole in a consciousness crammed with ambiguities. Weary, Camomille gives her hide a little stretch. Points her breasts skyward and takes a deep breath. Smiles. Thinks *feel okay* like a fan spread but in no hurry to cool a whole room. Sponge rubber sponge, the waiter's hand, wrist, sleeve. He brushes against the table. Scratches his cheek. Clears the table. Glasses.

So we're afloat between two generations of drinkers ————————

————————————————————————————

——— a floating city, Montgolfier's balloon, up and up to touch the blue and dizzy turns, turning upside down; puffy clouds race by, dip and scud against the rocks, the river below. The plunge. Yes we've turned upside down.

Head downward and plenty of concepts stirring there, concentrating denser and denser in a single meditative strategy.

Not much noise in this joint at this hour of the afternoon.

Titubating tongue.

On cheek close to lips, on brow beside the eyes, she moistens, turns
——————————— soft, dissolves faces.

Gives me visions of ramifying cells, others coming loose under the mouth's roof, green ones with yellow nuclei, blue ones following closely in the text your mouth    the city full of shadow creatures with the fall of night; pinball machines, juke box, bar, grill. All the other side of the coin too of course; the kitchen and a game of patience, the TV, the bedroom – won't sleep much between now and tomorrow morning.

Or else, so anxious to nullify oneself, one explodes in the other's mouth. Point blank.

So the kiss will have been a rerunning of the gauntlet before a mirror, a puckering of lips, a total opening, an uncontrollable plunge. If twisting your wrists to make you open your mouth and getting me inside helps to ventilate some fantasies, it's because the text itself begs for a possible intrusion and abuse of use that you'd fritter away some other way anyway;

Camomille, you've got to swallow / spit out the other. Exclude the too too obvious from your mouth in any case. Tongue oblique / over / the other tongue, make it circulate one way then the other, a whirlygig of duplication, complicity.

Bye-bye french kiss, go drag your stuff someplace else: the thought hangs on the tip of my tongue like a saliva drop, a checkered blob of false reality. Impression that your teeth are blowing on the window panes, that snow is falling, that fragments are breaking into silly little flakes, molecules and desire and also eager laughable snickering narrator, off her rocker in mirth. Literally infinitely fibs

flip-flops

brandishing suspended meanings. Which fall into place as fictional / real ———————— the other's mouth; Camomille disrobes in almost classic style, dress falling circular on the floor. Key. Click. Pale chic lipstick plastered everywhere blotting the landscape, the scenery. Special effects.

Such a kiss it will have been that neither the desire nor the saliva could have been more meticulously, tremblingly strewn inside your mouth, wherein to do the tour, idle round your mouthhole in the lower reaches of the city.

A FEW TIMES MORE
OR
*EXPENDITURE* FOR A SIGN
BECAUSE
*MORE* WILL BE EMBODIED WHERE
a signifier has been
*being deletable to your eyes*

No more sidetracks, two-pronged statements, forking off. Marielle's behind the wheel. Passes the Black Cat, junkie hangout and hot tin roof, galvanized. Psychedelic counterpane. Apartment house: five ten fifteen twenty floors, doorbell panel, carpeting, elevator, sun deck, pool. Incinerator.

The Main. Élysée Theatre. Ticket wicket lineup. Inner screen, positions social and erotic, politics, chocolate bars and Seven-Up. Pocket paperback what for?

Marielle crosses the Main, heading west along Sherbrooke Street, toward Bleury, Stanley. Passes within yards of 'her office.' Doesn't even look. Mind you.

* * *

Have to cut out the trite intrigues.

A trap. The city's soul divided, clove in two. In its middle, moans. Having been caught. Henceforth in its double depths of memory, the double centre of a double city, there's east and west and between the twain. And pain. Several verbs before being caught short. For having taken leave of our tenses.

Marielle passes a bus full of people with faces all in a row pressed against the windows. Confused mass of heads and brou ha ha. Walking laundry bags. All hangs on a very simple image of preshrunk brains. Washed, pressed and some OD'ed.

* * *

Repetitions issue from my mouth like lots being drawn. A lot of echoes. A rush of relapsed words. Recidivate the better to disturb. A right of retort to Camomille's kiss, to the uncertain route being taken by Marielle.

I doze, catnap, fantasize and am Lucy's double. Words and trickitis – pardon, trichites, hairlike crystals in my head. Sherbrooke Street a thread of stability with a defective yarn. Reds, greens. Passersby implanted at every intersection.

Slow down the mechanism, the gear-grinding of heavy footsteps on cement, the many sounds an eardrum receives and amplifies. Muscles move and are spent like tissues of lies; their fibres activate, fomenting desire for comment. True narrative. Consider the meaning of occurrences. The root source of a show.

* * *

or reproduction. A riposte that's integrated with a reading / critique. The disarray that's inflicted on the table of contents, the seed that's sown when one sees how lovingly the trick's been played – to get one's vulva to turn, the way they say the dead turn over in their graves, face down. Buttocks to the sky.

Stir the pot. With all the hand's furthest extremities, reproduce oneself from the soles of one's feet to the roots of one's hair, with quote marks all over to make sure every meaning gets its due. Instigating points. Inter / text. Queries reaching citywards. So as to tell the insipid from the sapid in case the meanings make off, go off the track. In the most complete confusion. To wit, why does this painful game go on, dangling like a pencil from one's fingers?

* * *

The why would ease Marielle's knuckles, white round Violet's steering wheel. This is the English Sherbrooke Street, productive, g'dammit, and laid out in fog and cold sweat.

In this context everything proliferates and operates. As though shifts of meaning to be lifelike must have been made roughly and improperly.

Constant thrashings over. An action-packed book. Rip into this texture. Tear open a passage for Marielle.

Discriminate.
    breakthrough
        Diverge
since confluence has taken place. Just once.

Penetrate.
Make openings.

* * *

In the city's very heart but
what for?
Alien and target
roundabouts
TRAFFIC
bump and grind an opening

TO MEANING

Our mouths recharge full with predilection for salt and edibles on the tongue. Taste. A whole miraculous world of pleasure since to have taste one must be full of tenderness, of furor catapulting to a state of consciousness. Contact with. Caught in its current, flow.

Loss of one's notion of time far from shore yes the sea decomposes images.
Elle is with her other body.

* * *

For a polemical existence. Series of feet sticking out to trip, projections on / into the landscape of the city. Voice inflexions to prevent the night from advancing imperiously pale over Montréal, as neon signs hard-outlined on the eye wink on and off. Fresh – THE SHOW MUST GO ON BUT

The narrators pucker like shivering people all crumpled up. The retinal night: pleasure and laughter in a bold-faced letter against the shadows and image play which make the eye see Nadja / Diane Dufresne screwing (making rhyme and reason). Textually, to foil the reader-strategists, soundtrack and image spoilers as our slow-motion limbs direct. Dervish-whirling. Fever heat. Anamorphosis.

Mike, radio. Marielle on Sherbrooke Street. Not the slightest question of giving the gas the gun. Rain again.

* * *

They pucker up, skin creased all the way to their bucal membranes, makes it impossible to move their tongues so as to ar-ti-cu-late pre-cise-ly, 'How many peppers has Peter Piper picked? Peter Piper's picked a peck of pickled peppers.'

In their superheated state, their inconsequence, their eagerness flags and dies away. Lucy Lexa Camomille, fever heat rising to their cheeks but not high enough like a half-zipped fly, a thermometer showing fifty or so Fahrenheit. On Saint-Denis Street. Y'know how it is when ya got a pedigree. Saint-Louis Square. Mud pies and guitars. Pushher. RIGHT ON! Too Much!

Mishmash of ramifications. Tangled web.

The city collapses in the west and downtown, lungs larynx, mouthorgan blues. Far off – seven bus stops farther on – Montréal passes out. Westward.

* * *

# CHAPTER I

Five of us there were to share that happy time. We knew and roamed all the city's arteries in ourselves. For years we'd been turning more kaleidoscopes than there really are. Working alone each in our own way. Then one day things happened. We resolved to give ourselves a break, and try to live each for ourselves in the body of each other one. So began our evolution.

We wanted and expected more and more each time we found

that everything was revolving round ourselves as stimulants, oracles of truth. And our collective inclinations stirred us with sensitivity and tenderness. With happiness. Whenever we'd meet on Colonial Street looking for (and finding) delight. From 1973 to '78, a lot of words got lost, went astray in every sense (Lucy then had flung herself with wild abandon into writing, burned and burning with creative fire. Little by little she won possession of the image and epidermis, the 'certainty of body' that was Camomille, whom she'd met by chance on Mykonos. Amid the vivid too-blue-to-be-true of the sea and setting suns. No one could interrupt the bewitchment and explorations of the pair. Except for Georges and Alexandre. But the game they played was most ambiguous, as though they periodically detached themselves from the scene of Montréal to celebrate a kind of second state untouched by context of any kind).

In the setting of Lucy's book.

At the time, we were stirring more matter than all the scientists on earth in unison. The world kept coming unstitched and we never had too little thread to close the gaping seams to our advantage, as it suited us. Depending on what urges were taking charge of us.

The city in reduced scale. The city moves in one's eye as fast as Nick Mason's acrobatic drumstick on his drums, at Pompei. A shadow of doubt glows crimson over passersby, falls on them. Soot, sequel, footsteps, Lasalle taxicabs. All drift, not significantly but with the city setting, flow toward the port the docks the river under Victoria Bridge.

Alexandre turns to look at Georges who's following with Lucy. Wheels squeal, teeth close inside one's mouth, look for a tongue to bite, get a hold and a bird in the hand and. Snow too perhaps for chapping lips, splitting them, cracking like two matches when they light.

The body moves up Saint-Denis Street, feet sloshing through the slush, like a spermatozoon with propelling tail. Wends a sense. Cell.

* * *

The traffic lights aren't synchronized. Change of gear. The city's still the city but it's foreign. Inset plate, breather for narrators. Inset mouth. Distorted like a doctored income tax return. A fuddled blotting-paper document. Ink soot saliva. Camomille you make me make such curious progressions – thrice armed I ride grammar, you're forcing the body and the I (another reason for hallucinating cells, molecules, atoms, blank text). The galaxy takes me off guard being the subject of the present sentence. Present unaccounted for and a yen for travel. In the fabric, all possible routes.

Foot hard on the brake chrr-eish!

* * *

Curl up like an alibi in the sentence to lift one's stomach, entice it to let itself go, but utterly – the wanting muscle, radar guide in the depths of one's flesh. The furrows, tracks in the palm of that hand rivetted to the steering wheel, the obedient wheel turning hardly at all, steering Marielle straight ahead. Guy Street, Montréal Seminary, grounds green and deep, nun's convent next. Sherbrooke Street Englisher and Englisher and noisy like a big barnful of ornery cattle.

Turn now to a reality other than the obvious one. Cut the civil and trite intrigues. Featherweights and heavy with aggression. Open the valves. Awareness. Trigger it. Love me love my body Camomille, with exploration. Geography / show featuring the city. A lengthy irrigation through each vein. An intravenous penetration of cities and highway systems. But cut the trite intrigues.

* * *

There's a triggering technique that gets the words in motion round Marielle; roar of engines, shifts of vowels, analogies breed, parachutes open, feathers and flirtations fall on blank white spaces.

They switch direction. REVERSE. BACK UP. R. REAR. Marielle backs into a system of contracting and decontracting muscles. Pedestrians fictional and textual, some shivering as they wait for the bus. Muscles push and pull, muscles triumph.

On the sidewalk, the snow writhes as it melts. Salt. Calcium. Victoria Hall, Grosvenor Street. Men are stooping, seasoning the road with salt. No one wants to talk.

* * *

Cross the blank white zone that marks the demarcation between Marielle Elle and Marielle Desaulniers, switchboard operator, hairdresser, WAITRESS, dancer, salesgirl; woman with hair dyed blue. Jade blue and hocus pocus … see there and in the ball crystal-clear reflections globule words, the way life is in and out and round about the choppers in a mouth, poking into cavities.

That gentle way one has at the centre of oneself, as if moved by a gentle muscle turning out to be all love and love alone inside the heart the heart. With lots of meaning outlets.

Next there comes pro / pulsion. Effervescence. Dilated words. Elle pulls out and passes a Volks. A tempting beard. Her eye swerves under its lid as if for a rendez-vous. Perspectives.

* * *

Traffic heavier where Sherbrooke meets the Decarie autoroute. An interchange going nowhere in all directions. Stir the autobodies rocking reeling swinging partners fishtails on the ice, frost. Crazy crates, diverted by some disruptive magnetism from their paths.

Going nowhere. Thoroughly upset. (narrative / continuity). Smash skulls as in an abattoir, brains (all distortion) so vulnerable, sapwood without sap ... but dreams, molecular chains. Proteins.

Leaving the text, sinking back in would bring forth another figure, or disappearing, then to move under the surface with wing-like texture to confront reality. Would sharpen the lines or confuse the whole with pleasure (bring together / split the cells) an insinuating cleft marvellous for darting through. Thrust aside all powers outside the text – breathe a word between those legs and break through / free

One fell swoop of the screen and space for connivance sweeps over all the regions of the body losing / winning, separation from the body, hovering over one's own body system.

* * *

Pull away with the thought and sensual impression that all the body's cells are floating back through history, transforming to nerve fibres, streaking through space heedless of inside or out, space before the expulsion.

Marielle finds as of now she's feeling the pull of a sustained urge, to sink into the text with all the connections possible through passion's transport and lucidity. Join the filaments of life with fluid and you get the matrix of animation.

Rain. Almost snow. Mongrel pentagonal flakes. Gray pantomime. Sherbrooke Street in any season, any direction. No compensation. The city in neutral gear. Then jammed rough like into [—] icy metal ice.

* * *

Pangs: the other's tongue, astride in control in the mouth, stretches out then lies still like a ribbon come to rest on a plot of grass. Somewhere on Saint-Denis Street, Georges and Alexandre try drinking shots, thimblefuls – 'If there were no space between matter all the human race would fit in a thimble' – spinning the barrel, counting the chance, getting into it (a corridor for a fairy finger spinning and keeping clear of the needle point). Here shadows and racing pulses copulate, slip durable one into the other like the images in binoculars of blinding power.

Through all this sequence showing Georges and Lexa (snack bar, full licence, meat balls hot dogs ice cream sundaes) we discern the city's details and its cracks.

The photogenetic click.

* * *

Sequel and provocation. Repeated waving grasses on the retina. The eye wavers in its orbit in its spaceship then takes off at the speed of light. Street lamps, neon signs, the movie shows round town. The eye turns on itself, a reference point on the nervous surface of this body in transit.

Marielle's decoding in her hellcat's heap, a purple carbuncle on the English gray face of hallucinated buildings along Sherbrooke Street:

Words woo you in courtly style. Beaten track.

We flounder in grand scale down that damn great swath of pavement that's drawing to an execrable end like the archives of our history. Elle takes off

old yellowed book. Pages one by one.

* * *

The subject's in sight but
doesn't spread itself or otherwise

The network interferes with intersecting differences. The mesh. Streets and arteries, traps or else the ropes in city planning.

Marielle's gaze spills weariness on the autumn gardens. The light reminds her of a rainy early morning at Lanoraie. But it's five o'clock and in November an afternoon is short. Disturbing in the black, the white, a Giguère-inspired museum. Lines and wisdom in rounds and curves.

* * *

Page one to … grab that page on the fly as it slips away in / to the light. A journey / a reading. The stuff of the page analogous to pleasure in the senses, in directions (west / east: breakout into open space, effusion), in the sense of whatever it is that's lost upside downside another dimension, otherwise.

Page let loose. Camomille, dispersion crazily with her tongue. She who has broken and entered to explore, having run out of excuses to get her teeth into, masks of living burning skin, henceforth will have to feed on her own pleasure machine, all those cells like shimmering comet tails in her brain.

* * *

At the other end of the city, near Cherrier Street, houses, roofs, facades, walls, verandas, front stoops, tiny plots of grassless earth; local tavern, convent, institution. Godawful place. Kitchen. Space reduction.

Home in the kitchen on Colonial Street we tilt and rock our chairs and ruminate the direction / meaning of this long drive by our little big sister Elle. Together we agree on marvellous things, listen to each other tilting chairs and fantasies. Chemical / electrical bodies canting oblique substances. Canticles and linoleum all well-worn.

O Holy Night on a gray November afternoon. On course for infractions.

Fixed smiles to swap for Vaseline, anus lubrication. Conductive ointment. Encephalogram. Those waves plugging together, leaping through your directions! Your zoo of love, reader. Acrobatics.

* * *

Let's say Marielle's been lulling herself with anecdotes and radio on Sherbrooke Street and now casts her eyes on the beginning of the beginning of the end of that long, long street. As it happens, the décor's in disguise. Christmas tree colours and gobs of blue-gray great for hair dye. Marielle gnaws at her nails, worries at her brake. Feels Dracula lurking in the November dusk. Though the English have a sweet tooth for ghosts. A trick of inner discourse. Coax out words with which to talk back to the echo in one's throat, hark back to the early morning hours like an illegal level of noise suddenly confronted with legal polluted air.

* * *

Let's say she feels like a fiction laboratory where breaths balloon, knees jerk and nerves are skin deep, then the index shows promise. Life skids against the slippery sides

Parasitic static noise. Must stand out from the rest. A sentence unfin          A sentence of pure fiction that's hard to bring to life with images and comparisons. An atmosphere unstitched. Cutting words. Scraps. Attend to them in enticing pose, showing curiosities. Conspicuous. How to get enough when hallucinating on the fermentations of content going on. All-embracing form. Projection.

HOLOGRAM

of test tubes. All leads are for exploring, also the other's very absolute desire which is dissolving bit by bit, and the self, a roll of dice so absolute it turns in my belly like a genetic code crammed with equations and curves to infinity.

say she's listening to herself talking to herself inside the four walls of her car. Say we're seeing Violet telescoped in a potential news item in Marcil Park, in which Elle parks in front of the Cinema V, gets out and goes into a small chips and bubble gum store. Comes back out holding a bottle of Orangeade. Crosses the street. Sits on a bench in the gray park with autumn trees behind. And falls asleep.

Potential news item: woman with psychedelic blue hair, Orangeade – colours in a space; round Elle, two / three freaks orbiting, angel faces Gilmour style, some soft caresses with a palm, flat of a hand.

Electric my blue-haired sleeping beauty. HONEY CAN YOU SPARE A BUCK? She's woken. Stretches, very nervous fibre as far as Violet. Departs. And, in her soul, goes back to sleep stepping on the gas. A BUCK'S A BUCK. The forest, a stately denizen.

* * *

As for the text's intention or deviation, she's got it on the brain. Perdition from one word to … the next, letter for … Narrators and lenses. Memory: much more than remembering Lucy and Georges, the summers at Lanoraie, the winters in N.D.G., the 'highs' on Colonial Street, Violet's brand new tires, Camomille's long French kiss ———————————— DNA, the code, galloping queenly substances, the bodies that started it all. The white centre. Understanding is a sojourn. The story I have to tell, the furthest reaches, a version of love.

A lead.
To be followed or

take-off

The eye's overindulging tonight / this morning / tonight, gorging on functions of pleasure to be found, of ecstasy in – here leave some syllables dangling the blue of your eyes juana. All over the place.

* * *

Return trip back and forth between the west end and Colonial Street. Montréal comes apart, is swallowed, a gray pill and climate of uncertainty. The streets and boulevards pump soot, mud, slush all the way to Central Station. In left field, marshalling yards: a train going somewhere, a Rapido coming sometime soon. Railway ties like sutures in the earth.

The métro's full to bursting. The car doors open, gobble, then hush their chatter bit by bit down the black hole. Other ramifications. Under the city. Over, criss-cross of helicopters. Radio, police taking the pulse of the fabric, the plastic, the brick, the bric-a-brac and *crazier than Braque's foetus in a cube*.

The city white hot in the gray. What time is it? Chimneys are puffing puking smoke upward like winter's rigours, gassing a whole city as it goes to sleep cosy warm and unconcerned.

* * *

## CHAPTER II

Alexandre was madly in love with his sister Marielle. He'd never been able to understand why everything went on in him as though he wasn't free to stop loving the woman who, as he said himself, was really pretty ordinary. After all. For him it certainly wasn't just a magical mystery love.

By 1973, Montréal for us was finished with. A city that had nothing left to say to us. There came a point where Lucy thought she'd try exploring it from stem to stern, see what it would stimulate, becoming one with it house by house, a patch of shadow or a patch of wall. She swelled up with analogies before our eyes. At the drop of a hat she'd trip off to the farthest reaches of her soul.

So we were happy all this time, like believers taking first communion. Affectionate celebrants. Orgiasts. Searchers without precise aims. Prospectors for that seam of gold. The one obsession we couldn't escape was the city and its streets, which we roamed on foot, by bus, by taxi, in Violet with all her giddy turns along the way. Pranksome car. Once we rented three motor bikes for two days. We roared athrob all over the place. Potholes, oily patches on the pavement, perilous pebbles in back lanes. Marielle, alone on her bike one day, invited a little tyke of ten to ride behind her and all day long he stayed with us, leading us to discoveries. Spaces. Quarry in two senses. Sand.

We had an impression five years long that someone was telling us a story. One we believed. We filled the gaps and scratched out the repetitions that didn't suit our exploratory wants.

What our bodies did and how they worked fascinated us as well.

None of us were ever sick through those five years. But we felt, or rather we were sure we knew our bodies, exploring every last recess. To the very core. In pleasure and in pain, when for example we didn't realize one's body could feel orgasms suddenly and *incidentally*. That nipped in the bud our blossoming to realities that were new. Ones already there. But for us still new, enigmatic, erectile ones.

In 1977, Marielle had a child by Alexandre. At first we thought that would end it all. That we'd go back to what we'd been. Back to our offices and factories. All five of us were present for the birth. Two li'l daddies, two li'l mammies, we bawled like frightened kids while Marielle breathed in and out, blowing her best on that ember of life. Her contractions, rhythms, relaxations.

Elle and Lexa weren't a couple. We were a fivesome. Utopians living on the fringe, roving full of dash and flash, feeling life and all its secretions moving inside of us. The inner alchemies left us limp with willingness.

Yet there came a time of some anxiety. Reality was slipping from our grasp. Fiction was taking hold of us. Like a spell. What magic potion had we drunk? Or was it Montréal that kept changing and making us think it was one long hallucination we were in?

Enlarge the structure of things. Explore them. Through and through. A celebration of festive epidermises. A peacock fan open then closed, a multiplicity of facets on a film. A process that tends to open up the senses and meanings too. The storied glory of the body. Its smile is chemical above all. Its illumination ———

——— In orbit, revolution round the body / text. The earth turns. The blue of it is not at all like an orange. Something to be probed anew like a layer of history.

An episode of concentration on the curious eye of a mutant that's barely visible. Already yet. For the text is a perpetual search. Therein each avenue, deletion and line intersecting, interpreting itself. From now on it's outside the patchwork lexicon cut from historic angst. Afloat and expanding if possible. The writing / neuron and connection through fibres, synapses. Transvibrations. Atmospheric tensions (reproduction / dissemination) soothed. Handle our words like the alchemist's gold we traffic in, conjunction or dispersion of arguments.

If. Since with Violet (Marielle inside) we could cross through spaces and confuse the time with the ties of desire ('ties me in knots not understanding you'). If joining together in the content, ritual or real / fictional – on back breasts eyes, inside the mouth – animates the neuron and includes it, that's perfect joining, utopia, in each of the body's cells and .......... its correspondent in the text. Though often one excludes the other.

Enlargement of the species. Marielle's frizzed-up head of hair.

* * *

You pull up and knot your scarf with the orange palm trees on. Your fantasy over the N$^{th}$ parallel. But also the napalm in your hair raven blot on the century.

Transports one since things are changing bit by bit in Marielle's car and bean. After all that driving round and scraping on walls and motifs.

Leaving the city, now, by Route 2, heading for Mercier Bridge. Its rusty old steel and worn white lines. Out of line. The blackness of the blue. The river and the Caughnawaga *Reserve*. Châteauguay, its church, the patriotes. The past. But cut the trite intrigues so the roles, tragedies, *revolting* things won't be dragged out.

Capsules in orbit. Each independent at its core.

Transports one and blurs this era of paradox. Smears colours on the worn linoleum where Alexandre and Lucy are swapping tales of souls returned and *patriotes* in warm wool tuques. Once upon a time. Nagasaki or somewhere in Québec, villages scrambled in the ink of history. Evergreens and orange trees. Kimonos and flannel nightshirts. The atom wipes out hiding places, spins redhanded in vital space, spins and spins. Supersonic Damocles. 'The spectacle of the event remains sealed in them.' The eye explodes in the microscope.

Wily is the eye which seeks in another's words and attitude what is to come in a story that doesn't stop at that                    so suddenly.

Pedestrian. The man in the street is a specimen of history.

## CHAPTER III

We were juggling reality and it frightened us. Ours was a never-never world that we knew just wasn't there. Urban science fiction turning us on and off. Ambulant switches, that's what we were.

That was when we began to see things from points of view that were different. Each day we'd turn up a list of words new to us. Words, objects, phantasms all lungs and respiration. Impulses. Protoplasm-girdled words. And with our phantasms, the splendid images we had of things.

Like control words we resisted the momentum drawing us in, dooming us to come to life in ourselves, to exist only in ourselves, each a soundless flute. Why? How hard it was to understand. To overcome our fear. To hold the universe in a single capsule on our tongue. Then swallow it. And die and die again with pleasure. A wild expansion of our consciousness. A flow, a thread. Relevance to.

Montréal, Camomille, Lexa, constant whirl. Maelstrom. We

questioned everything, passersby, neon signs, traffic, highrises. Eh! taxi! We had no choice by now. Launched as we were on a course of life and breath: question / breathe / inspire / expire, absorb you, combine you, melt you, cell of love. All the living fish species from Australia, Africa and the Americas glided by in pageantry before our eyes. In full pollution. Panoramic screen.

Most of all Montréal was a sensory experiment in which we'd test ourselves, looking for a rhythm, a perfect (total) usage of our bodies, viscera, epidermises.

Our ambulant nervous systems were turning us outside in, behind the window-dressing which was our programming. One could rightly say we were recharging our batteries.

As the third year ended, we sensed that we should talk in other ways about an other thing, for us akin to pleasure and delight. It was difficult and soon everything became equivocal. How far might we go? Could we stop? How would it all come off? We were questions and participation both at once, for none of us – despite the *testing* – wanted to stop at the point where all in life was self-evident and self-propelled. We were radars terrified by the signals we were capturing beneath the celestial dome. Our nerve fibres played like virtuosi with the hammering they took. We were terrified and comfortable.

Then gradually we got control of most of our interventions. Our part in reality was that we weren't taken in by anything. At least we managed to communicate among ourselves all the fragments of knowledge and wisdom each of us had access to from our own enquiry and experience. We were awareness and communication.

Sometimes we read marvellous texts which enthralled us still, though we were certain of living today outside the text (we led each other without pushing to think *differently* about all the body's energy exchanges and expenditures, connections, seas of tranquility. Mutation.

We perceived things in a way so utterly unheard of that at times we thought we might be going mad. But there again, we'd have to know what madness was, its surface manifestations, its others so deep down. Strangling feelings in the breast. In that sense Camomille was an easy prey. Her uncontrollable energy expenditure.

In 1978, at the very beginning of the year, some Island of Montréal Urban Community policemen came to Colonial Street and smashed everything. Our most valuable equipment. Our documentation. Then it was that Lucy began to write again for a while, long enough to liquidate the violent body whose terrorist mania was for tilting at all civil / social taboos. Her mission was to cut out trite intrigues so we could remake our laser beams. Energy and meditation. Satisfy our bodies and awareness till we could take no more.

In May of that year Georges learned chinese and English and some other languages. The purpose of the exercise seemed obscure and Georges died and said nothing that might enlighten us.

But we were on his heels, pursuing him in everything he read, though he could follow all the forms a text might take and understand them too, slick them across a retina like magic oils, psychedelic inks, such machination and enchantment in an eye. While on the back of his reek graphic shadows fell like gentle morning rain

in May of that year,

And fragments in the city.

Focus trained on collective individuals who cluster as Siamese or Centumese, scary octopi outside the insides of movie houses. Close-up: man-in-the-street stares stubbornly into a glass. Turns his kaleidoscope. Lights. Turn-on. Multifarious variants spring forth. All of us focus on our own nebulae. With eyes peeled, dig into those heaps of stellar dust. Inside our breasts and over all the surface of our bodies, bite into life as into an apple in paradise regained. Contact. Mucous membranes that tally. The man-in-the-street's walking differently now. Discover his bio / chemical angel architecture through an elliptical glass that gives him back a neurological reflection of the species (Narcissus was no swimmer you know).

* * *

It's dark. Six in the evening. December magic. Evergreens, naked trees (maples, oaks … ). Elle has left Violet parked, goes to walk a while in a funny little wood behind the big shopping centre in Châteauguay. Lights faint not far. It's snowing a bit. Bing Crosby dreaming of a white Christmas. See the squirrel tracks. Dog tracks, cat tracks.

* * *

The dark of evening glides closer to the lens. Focusing consumes the fictional reality of night in gross photographic grains. Disarms it with winking eye. Understanding is biding a while in an eye. In orbit among desirous cells, connectors of delights, beyond the certainty of not dying when suddenly the lights go on.

In pleasure spread.

Darkness on Colonial Street. Someone's turned out the light the better to see the snowflakes fall and hear the smallest sound. The better to understand why it's so right to see the neighbouring balconies turn white. A shovel grates on pavement. Night sequesters all dimensions till tomorrow. *My visions of a rising sun. Light of dawn. Scrambled shadows.* Night, the galaxy. Lexa Lucy Camomille Georgraphy are part of it all.

The network.

Their astrologer magus cards spread out on the arborite kitchen table top.

* * *

In Lucy's wandering reverie, the eager eye closes on a void (thinking about La Tuque (signifier) or Tarantula) instead of Mecca, runs out of steam in the middle of a sequence. A black hole of repose. Encircling radiant white. Inside myself I fly off in all directions. 'I've Got You Under My Skin,' sememes overshooting the mark. Wander beyond the historical mechanics in this chemical galaxy. The brain is something else. A 747 bound for Mecca. Atlases come alive in a field of plasma. Says Lexa, no one's going to tell their dreams unless it's to get excited over other things and find themselves new tides to ride. Asymbolic currents.

* * *

Not all versions can be right. No more than any one. And does the matter matter? Let's get our east-west orientations straight. Reset the setting.

Squander our reserves of meaning on real growing things and in certain gardens. Though it all comes to the same end in the end.

Now for the first time we're getting past analogies, getting to the central point of life. Getting inside a cell and living dying there. All vibration.

What's left for our story is to break up and be lost. Caughnawaga's underbrush. *Expenditure* for a sign. While death so soon obliterates our vanities / reflections, our historic reference points already lost in an agglomeration of shattered meanings. Montréal surface and totems: 'And in the middest of those fieldes is the sayd citie of Hochelaga, placed neere, and as it were ioyned to a great mountaine that is tilled round about, very fertill, on the toppe of which you may see very farre.' Dislocated cosmogony. SIGHTSEEING. Neon as far as the I can see. Flip out under one's pal.

She rides eager astride the delible ink.

## Editor's Note

As Coach House Books makes these groundbreaking works of experimental writing available again, we have taken the opportunity to correct errors in the original editions of the English translations. Most of these are minor – spelling mistakes, typographical errors, inconsistencies – but we have also, in consultation with Patricia Claxton, made two more substantial corrections: the omission of the final words in both panels of the comic strip in 'Nine Times' (pages 250–251 of *French Kiss*) and the incorrect ordering of sections in pages 294–296 of *French Kiss*. All corrections have the full approval of the author and the translators. With the above exceptions, the texts appear here exactly as they did in the original Coach House Press Quebec Translations editions.

– Alana Wilcox

## About the Translators

PATRICIA CLAXTON has translated a third novel by Nicole Brossard, *Baroque at Dawn* (*Baroque d'aube*), besides the two in this volume. Her translations include works by Gabrielle Roy, Jacques Godbout and François Ricard, and most recently *A Sunday at the Pool in Kigali* by Gil Courtemanche. She has twice received the Governor General's Award for Translation, in 1987 and 1999. She lives in Montréal.

LARRY SHOULDICE, 1945–1991, translated another book by Nicole Brossard, *Daydream Mechanics* (*Mécanique Jongleuse*). He also translated works by Donald Smith, Jacques Ferron, Alain Grandbois and Guy Corneau. His extensive literary criticism has appeared in such publications as *Canadian Literature, The Globe and Mail* and *The Oxford Companion to Canadian Literature.* Larry Shouldice was a professor of English literature at the Université de Sherbrooke.

## About the Author

NICOLE BROSSARD was born in Montréal in 1943. Poet, novelist and essayist, she has published more than twenty books since 1965. Among these are *These our Mothers, The Aerial Letter, Lovhers, Mauve Desert, Baroque at Dawn, Installations* and *Museum of Bone and Water*. By her ludic, subversive and innovative work on language, Brossard has influenced a whole generation on the questions of post-modernist and feminist writing. She also co-founded the important literary periodicals *La Barre du Jour* (1965) and *La nouvelle Barre du Jour* (1977). In 1976, she co-directed the film *Some American Feminists*. She also published in 1978 with Coach House Press *The Story So Far 6* and in 1991 she coedited the *Anthologie de la poésie des femmes au Québec (1688–1988)*. Ms Brossard was twice awarded the Governor General's Award for poetry, in 1974 and in 1984. She has also received Le Grand Prix international du Festival de Poésie de Trois-Rivières twice, in 1989 and in 1999. In 1991 she was awarded le Prix Athanase-David, the most important literary prize in Quebec literature. She has a Doctorate *honoris causa* from the University of Western Ontario (1991) and from the University of Sherbrooke (1997). Her work has been translated into English, Italian, Spanish, German, Japanese, Norwegian and other languages. She is a member of l'Académie des Lettres du Québec and of the World Academy of Poetry. The American critic Karen Gould has written about her work, 'The contributions of Nicole Brossard to contemporary literature and literary theory and their inevitable intersection through feminism have been visionary.' Nicole Brossard lives in Montréal.

Typeset in Adobe Garamond and Gill Sans
Printed and bound at the Coach House on bpNichol Lane, 2003

Edited and designed by Alana Wilcox
Cover image is a photo still from *Tlön, or how I held in my hands a vast methodical fragment of an unknown planet's entire history* (2003), an installation by Christine Davis
Photo of *Tlön* by Peter MacCallum
Permission to use this still generously given by Christine Davis
Cover design by Rick/Simon
Author photo, page 349, by Caroline Hayeur

Coach House Books
401 Huron Street (rear) on bpNichol Lane
Toronto, Ontario
M5S 2G5

416 979 2217
1 800 367 6360

mail@chbooks.com
www.chbooks.com